By: Rebecca Gober & Courtney Nuckels

Clean Teen Publishing

THIS book is a work of fiction. Names, characters, places and incidents are the product of the authors' imagination or are used factiously. Any resemblance to actual persons, living or dead, business establishments, events or locales is entirely coincidental.

NO part of this book may be reproduced, scanned, or distributed in any printed or electronic form without permission. Please do not participate in or encourage piracy of copyrighted materials in violation of the author's rights. Purchase only authorized editions.

ENDING ELE

Copyright ©2013 Rebecca Gober & Courtney Nuckels

Cover Design by: Marya Heiman
Typography by: Courtney Nuckels
Editing by: Cynthia Shepp

For more information about our content disclosure, please utilize the QR code above with your smart phone or visit us at

www.cleanteenpublishing.com.

ONE

The sound of a log losing its hearty fight against the raging fire startles me awake.

My heart is racing, but I don't know why. I refuse to open my eyes, worried that I'll see the stark fluorescent lights and grey concrete walls of a place I vaguely remember. A terror strong enough to taste fills my senses. The memory of what it is that I'm afraid of is hidden in the furthest recesses of my mind. I try to grasp ahold of it in hopes that the fear will dissolve when I recognize what it is that scares me. The search for the memory feels like swimming through a foggy ocean, which causes my head to pound.

The panic dissipates when I force myself to open my eyes and I see the wooden rafters of Tony's cabin. I blink my eyes a few times, trying to force the exhausted haziness from my vision. I look over at the piece of wood that has fallen through the grate in the fireplace. It morphs into brilliant, orange-red glowing embers. My heart rate steadies out as I watch the embers slowly progress to nothing more than grey ash.

The steady rise and fall of Tony's breathing behind me, comforts me. *He's here and I have nothing to fear,* I remind myself. But deep down, I know that there is a darkness making its way towards us and there is only so much time left before it swallows us whole.

"Don't think about it—not today," Tony says to me in our special form of mind speak, which only the two of us share.

I want to ask him what it is that I shouldn't think about, but I don't. Instead, I decide to relish in this moment. To allow myself to feel safe and secure with his warm arm draped across my middle. To memorize the way my head fits perfectly under his chin. Suddenly, I feel as if we aren't close enough. The stubble on his cheek tickles my forehead as I look up at him. His eyes are still closed and he looks endearingly innocent in his partial slumber. I stretch up and give him a small kiss on his sleeping lips. He smiles and his eyes flutter open. I can't get enough of those eyes, with the colors that mimic mine so perfectly. They are still a deep navy blue that leaves me trying to remember when he last healed, but the memory evades me. The prism of other colors are still visible when the light hits them just right and the ever-present red fleck sits towards the inside portion of his irises.

"Morning," he says aloud in a scratchy voice.

I can't help but feel a longing to hold him closer, to somehow become a single entity. "Morning," I say before I brush my lips against his once again. This time his lips crush into mine as he melts into our kiss.

"Happy Valentine's Day," Tony tells me.

I look at him confused. *Is it Valentine's Day already?*

I wonder. For some reason, this seems odd and out of place, like time passed without me being aware of it.

Tony gives me a half grin. *"You don't even remember the big day of love?"* He chuckles more so to himself, as if I amuse him in a completely adorable, loving kind of way.

I shove his chest lightly in a playful gesture. "With all that's been going on, I'm surprised you remembered."

"Actually, Sabby reminded me. He said I better get you something good." He winks at me.

That startles me into a new dimension of reality. I dart up from the couch and my heart starts racing as I look around the empty living room. "Where…?"

Tony is in front of me before I can complete my question. He braces me with his hands on my shoulders. "Whoa, it's okay, Willow. They're safe, remember?"

My eyes are wide as I stare at him. *No, I don't remember.* I keep the thought locked away.

Tony raises his eyebrow at me. "He's with the others—he's safe." Tony raises his hand to my forehead as if checking for a fever.

I don't stop him. Instead, I stare at the reflection of my silver eyes in the decorative mirror hanging on the wall, just behind Tony.

Tony moves into my line of sight, blocking my view of the mirror. He looks worried. "Willow, are you okay?"

"I'm not sure," I stutter. "This all…It seems so surreal. Like something is not quite right," I answer honestly.

"That's probably because nothing about these circumstances is right." He pulls me into him and I crush my face into his chest. The smell of earth and soap comforts me. "But I told you, we aren't going to think about that today," he reminds me, rubbing his hand across my back.

I nod my head against his chest and wrap my arms around him, holding him tightly. A twister of emotions stirs within me.

He gently pushes me from him just enough so he can see my face. He reaches his hand up and gently wipes a tear away from my cheek. I hadn't realized I was crying and I have no idea what's caused these feelings within me. "Why are you blocking yourself from me?" he asks, emotion apparent in his tone.

My stronghold crumbles as I realize what I'm doing. I drop the shield that I had not meant to put up in the first place. "I'm sorry," I tell him.

His face lightens when he sees the silver fade from my eyes. He kisses me on the tip of my nose and lets me go just long enough to place another log into the fire. The fire crackles and comes back to life. Pulling me back into his arms, he kisses the top of my head. He gently caresses my back with his hand, sending goose bumps down to my toes.

I feel his body shift as he brings my face up to his. "Will you come upstairs for a second? There's something I want to give to you."

I nod my head and give him a smile. He knows how much I like presents—especially from him.

He takes my hand in his and leads me to his parent's room. I look at him inquisitively as he opens the door and gestures for me to take a seat on the red chaise lounge near the bay window. I watch him in anticipation as he rummages through the closet. He removes a panel in the wall to reveal a safe. Excitedly, he turns to grin at me before he looks back at the safe and turns the dial several times. A second later, I hear a click as the safe is opened. While I can't see the contents, I can hear him shift papers and items around inside it before he carefully takes out a long, black box.

"Close your eyes," he says to me with a goofy grin.

I bite my lip but oblige. My legs bounce in anticipation as I hear him moving things around inside the black box. Then it snaps shut and I can hear him placing it back in the safe, securing it. The panel on the wall snaps back and I listen to him walk over to where I'm sitting. With my eyes still shut, he takes my hand in his.

"Can I open them now?" I ask impatiently. I like surprises but the wait is killing me. He doesn't answer me immediately and I get more fidgety. I can feel his palm sweating in my hand. *Why is he so nervous?* I think to myself.

"Okay, you can open them now," he tells me. His voice is soft, almost a whisper.

Now that the moment has come, I'm nervous too. I squeeze my eyes one last time and then open them. Tony is kneeling in front of me with my hand still in his. His other hand holds a small box and he places it in my lap.

My mouth goes dry and I suddenly forget how to speak. I blink a few times, trying to figure out what to do.

"Open it," he urges me. I take a deep breath and slowly remove the lid to the tiny box. Inside sits the most beautiful ring I've ever seen. My breathing goes ragged as I look back at him. My tongue is tied and I can't seem to speak. Instead, I hold his gaze, looking deep into his eyes.

Tony clears his throat. "Willow Mosby…" Just the way he says my name makes my heart get caught in my throat. "You mean everything to me; you're my whole world. My life begins and ends with you. After my parents died, I never thought I could love again, never thought I could be normal…until you came along. You turned my world upside down and taught me what it is to be a man. You showed me how to live and that love can happen, even in the darkest of times." He squeezes my hand in his. "I want you to have this ring, as a symbol of my love. I know that we're young, but I also know that a love like ours can only come along once and I don't want to ever chance losing it. I was going to give you this as a promise ring…a promise to you that we would someday marry. But the more I thought about it, the more I realized how badly I wanted it to mean more…now." The way he says 'now' makes my toes curl.

I suck in a breath at the realization of what he's about to say. His palm's hot in my hand, even though it is exceptionally cold up here. I swallow hard, waiting for him to say it.

"Willow Mosby, I want to spend the rest of my life with you. Would you do me the honor of becoming my wife?"

Tears spring to my eyes as the weight of what he just said sinks in. The expression on his face is so full of vulnerability that it makes me weep. I love this man in front of me all the way to the core of my being. But we are both still so young. What would my dad say? Then I understand what all this means. It means that Tony doesn't know what's going to happen from day to day. How much time we may have together…or lack thereof. But marriage? It's such a huge commitment and I'm not even a legal adult yet, and…and…I love him. I love him so much it hurts. I stare deeply into Tony's eyes. I can tell the silence is killing him. The uncertainty of my answer is like a half-ton weight sitting on his shoulders.

As he senses my hesitation, he adds, "Willow, we don't have to get married now, or in five years, or ten years. This ring signifies our love and commitment to each other. As much as it kills me to wait to become your husband, I'll wait as long as I have to. I owe you that much and you are worth every second."

A tear slips down my cheek as my heart soars. I purse my lips to keep from crying and nod my head. "Yes." My voice catches.

A huge smile spreads across his face and all the nervousness he was experiencing is now gone in an instant. He wastes no time taking the ring from the box and gliding it on my finger. As if he'd had it sized just for me, it fits perfectly. The other half of the ring lies in the box, the part I will receive when we say our vows. *I'm engaged*, I say over and over again in my mind.

"*We're engaged,*" he corrects me with a proud smile. Then he adds out loud, "This ring belonged to my mom. I brought their rings back here…after they died." This time his voice catches.

My eyes well with tears. That fact makes the significance of this gift all the more meaningful. I hold my hand up in the light and admire the stunning ring. It's platinum, set with a beautiful, princess-cut sapphire surrounded by six intricately cut diamonds.

I am immediately lost in Tony's arms, clinging to the man I deeply love. I don't want to let him go. I don't want to return to our reality. Then I'm flooded with grief. Grief about our situation, about how we may never remain alive long enough to get married. About how I'm only sixteen and no longer allowed to be a child, or allowed to grow up in a sheltered environment and have sleepovers with Claire—not allowed to ignore the danger that consistently lies all around us. The unfairness of it all angers me, but at the same time, Tony is making the best out of a difficult situation…and I love him for that.

The memory of something horrible tickles the edges of my mind. My hand starts shaking and Tony pulls me tightly to him. He pets my hair with his hand in a soothing gesture. "Don't think about it, Willow. Not today. Today is ours—not theirs. We won't let them take away this moment," he whispers into my ear.

Then I hear the sound of a door opening. Frosty air rushes over me and the world goes dark for a minute.

TWO

The frozen air sends a wave of icy shivers through my body.

Instinctively, I feel behind me for Tony but he's not there. I open my eyes to find him near the front door, taking off his snow-covered boots. His head lifts up and his gaze meets mine. His eyes brighten and a smile warm enough to melt away the cold crosses his lips. With a handful of logs in his arms, he quietly steps over my family and friends, who are spread out in front of the warm fireplace. He places the logs on the hearth, takes two of them, and sticks them into the fire. Then he turns to me.

Confusion washes over me as I recall the dream I was having before the cold air woke me. I look down at my dad and Sabby, who are sleeping soundly on the floor near my friends. The dream had felt too real. One minute I'm in Tony's arms and the next I'm waking up. It doesn't make sense. Then again, I've had enough visions to know that dreams aren't always just dreams.

Apparently, Tony notices that I'm lost in thought. He places his cold hands on my bare arms.

I almost squeal at the icy touch. "Cold," I tell him in a breathless whisper, careful not to wake anyone up.

Suppressing a laugh, he places his warm lips on mine. "Morning," he says on my lips.

Flashbacks from the earlier vision invade my thoughts again. "Hey, what day is it today?" With all that's been happening, I've completely lost track of time.

"December 12th, why?" He looks at me with his tornado eyes and I can't help but reach out and touch his cheek with the side of my hand.

Two months until Valentine's Day. Two months until…until I'm engaged? The thought makes me nervous and giddy at the same time. Then reality clouds my vision. Why was I so worrisome in the vision, if that's what that feeling was? Where did everyone go? Tony said they were safe…but were they really?

"Hey," Tony says, interrupting my thoughts. He places his hand on mine, the one that was caressing his face just moments ago. "What did you see?" he asks.

I stare at him, stunned for a second. "Huh?" I ask.

"Your eyes, they're copper," he says knowingly. "Did you have a vision? What was it?"

I blink a few times, not sure how to answer him. Instinctively, I throw a block up in my mind.

Tony looks taken aback at my sudden use of the shielding power, but what am I supposed to tell him? *Yes, I just flashed forward to Valentine's Day and guess what…I accepted your proposal to become your wife.* Yeah, that'll go off really well. Plus, would the proposal really be genuine if he already knows ahead of time that he's going to ask or that I'm going to accept? What if my vision prompts him to ask me the question? What if he doesn't really want to ask me to marry him but he feels compelled to because I'm already expecting it? I roll my eyes at the game of twenty-one questions that I seem to be playing with myself this morning.

"Are you okay, Willow?" Tony's look turns to worry, his eyes creasing in the middle.

I nod my head and try to soften the mood. "I had a strange dream. I don't remember much of it though." He doesn't seem to buy my excuse so I change the subject. "Hey, thanks for bringing in the wood. The fire was about to go out."

He eyes me for a second longer before he stands up and breaks the connection. Crossing over the sleeping bodies, he pokes the fire with the iron rod.

"It's cold out there," he says, making small talk. "Looks like we may get more snow." He can tell I'm hiding something but, thankfully, he doesn't pry.

Claire stirs next to me, followed by Connor. Soon, everyone is sitting up, rubbing their eyes. Connor's hair is sticking up every which way, with a handprint left on his face from how he slept.

"Hey hot stuff," I say, shooting him a grin.

The confused look he gives me is priceless. Claire seems confused until she looks at Connor. Pretty soon, we're giggling like schoolgirls. This wakes up Alec and Marya, which makes us laugh harder because Alec's hair mimics Connor's. Everyone is looking at us like we've lost our minds. Marya grins at us, understanding our inside joke. She playfully pats down Alec's messy bed head. He gives us a grimace when he sees we were laughing at his hair, the annoyance never reaching his eyes.

After a few minutes, the laughter dies down and we all fall into a quiet silence. My dad and brother are still heavily asleep. I stare at my dad with concern. His breathing seems labored and I can see his eyes moving back and forth under his eyelids. Every few seconds, he makes a spastic movement.

Eventually, my dad's unrest wakes Sebastian up just enough to crawl into my lap. He falls back asleep as he curls into my arms. I rub my hand across his curls. His hair is a lot longer now and I notice that it's losing the tight ringlets it once possessed. Now his curls are looser, making him look older. Like the five year old he's about to become. The thought reminds me—if today is December 12th, then that means Sebastian's birthday is in three days, on December 15th. I make a mental note to find a way to make it special for him.

With a heavy intake of air, my dad shoots up into sitting position. He breathes heavily as he looks about the room frantically from side to side. His eyes are glowing with intensity. They are a fiery pit of melted copper. His gaze finally lands on my brother and me.

"What happened? What did you see?" I ask in alarm. Knowing that a startling wake up like he just had has to mean he was in a deep vision entrancement.

"We have to go now! They're coming." With that, he jumps to his feet and grabs Sebastian's coat. I wake Sabby up and he gives us a grouchy look but doesn't say anything.

We don't wait to ask more questions. Within seconds, the room is one huge blur of frantic activity. Tony, who is already dressed for the cold weather, is stuffing food supplies, blankets, and flashlights in a duffle bag. "How much time?" he calls out to my dad, who is helping Sebastian get on his shoes.

I throw on my coat and take over, helping Sebastian so my dad can focus on answering.

"I don't know. With it being overcast outside, I couldn't tell the time of day. I know they will come when the sky is filled with snow. So much snow that we won't see them coming through the windows," my father says.

"Was it the soldiers, Dad?" I ask.

He blinks his eyes rapidly as if trying to put some pieces together. "No…" He runs his hands through his hair in frustration. "No, at least I don't think it was. They didn't have on any uniforms like the ones we saw last night. This was a smaller group but they came…" His eyes nearly fill with tears but he swallows the emotions down. "They came for you, Willow. They don't plan to take hostages. They just wanted you and were not going to let any of us stop them. They will use lethal force if necessary to achieve their goal." His gaze lands on Sebastian and I can only assume that something happened to my brother in that vision.

My heart lurches. How many times will my loved ones be put in danger because of me? Why do I keep putting them in this situation?

"You are not the one putting them in danger. The

ones who are against us are to blame. Don't confuse the two, Willow. You have done nothing to deserve any of this," Tony says inside my mind.

I finish tying Sebastian's shoes and look up to catch Tony staring at me from across the room. I merely nod, not convinced that everything he's saying is true. The danger has come to us *because* of me.

"*No, it's because of them,*" Tony demands. His face is full of emotion.

"*You don't always have to listen to my thoughts.*" I don't realize I'm glaring at him until his expression drops. Guilt rushes in and over me. "*I'm sorry Tony. I…I hate this. All of this!*" I gesture around the room. "*Running, we are always running.*"

He crosses the room swiftly, using his unearthly speed. I stand up when he reaches me.

"It won't always be like this. I promise. We will find a way in this crazy world. I promise you," Tony tells me in a whispered voice. He tenderly tucks a loose strand of hair behind my ear.

My eyes well up with tears and the emotion is thick in my voice when I say, "I hope so."

His hand rests on my cheek and for a moment, it's just Tony and me in this room. He leans in to kiss me.

"Ewwww! That gross!" Sebastian calls out before our lips meet.

We both let out an embarrassed laugh and look down at my little brother. His face is all scrunched up, like he smelled something horribly stinky.

Ending ELE

Tony ruffles Sabby's hair. "You won't always think that way, sport."

"Yes I will!" Sabby throws his hands on his hips and stands up tall, prompting another round of laughs from us.

"Let's move," my dad calls out from behind us. His voice holds a serious tone, reminding us of the severity of the situation. "Now!" With that call to action, the room is a blur of movement again. We grab our things and step out into the blustery cold together.

"The snow is picking up," Marya says. Alec instinctively drapes his arm around her.

When we're almost to the lake, I look back at the cabin. The snow is falling in thick sheets now. I can barely see the light from the fireplace at this distance.

Tony looks back at the cabin too. "They're here," he whispers.

Our whole group stops, crouching in the snow and we try to stare through the blizzard-like conditions. A black silhouette crosses in front of the lit-up window. We hold our breath as two more silhouettes walk to the front of the cabin. I can see the outline of the assault rifle hanging from one of their backs. We watch one of them kick open the front door. Two more large figures come up behind the group of three. Armed, they enter the cabin.

We should probably be putting some distance between the cabin and us, but something has us glued to this spot. We watch for several minutes as they search the cabin in silence. After a few minutes, a man steps back out into the cold. I can barely make out his frame but something about him is familiar. "Search the forest!" he yells to the others.

It was loud enough for us to hear his order from here. Alec and I turn to each other in the next instant. Recognition of that voice is clear in both of our expressions. This was no stranger hunting us. That was Alec's dad.

THREE

Without another word, we're on our feet and running.

With Claire and me keeping everyone invisible, we make our way around the lake and through the forest. Tony stays behind, wiping away our tracks in the snow. My dad guides us in the direction of the second safe house. We don't stop running until after a few hours have passed. We all take turns carrying Sebastian and doing our best to keep him warm. Needing to take a break, we stop behind a large grouping of evergreens. We listen intently for several minutes to verify that we weren't followed. Everyone takes the time to catch their breaths. A few of us take sips of water to make sure we stay hydrated.

I shiver as the sweat turns icy on my forehead. Tony throws his arm around me to lend me his warmth. My lungs feel like they have been cut up and down by the icy intakes of air I breathed during our quick escape. It takes only a few seconds and my healing ability for me to heal whatever parts of me are weary. I put my hand on my dad's shoulder and focus my healing on him. Alec and Tony catch on and do the same for the others.

With Sebastian being carried most of the way, he

seems to be fine but I put my hands on him anyway. He giggles a little. "That feel funny, Wello."

Although my stomach is still filled with the dread of seeing Alec's dad back in the picture, I manage to muster up a smile for my brother. I turn my attention to Tony and my dad, who are talking about the safe house.

"How much further do you think we have to go?" he asks my dad.

"I would guess we can be there within a few hours," my dad answers.

"Do you think the soldiers found that safe house?" Connor asks.

"I don't know. I haven't had any visions about it." He turns to look at me. "Have you, Willow?"

I blush and look down. I've had a vision, but not about the safe house. I look back at my dad and hope that he just assumes that my rosy cheeks are from the cold air hitting them. "I had a vision, back in the cabin. I didn't see anything about the safe house. I do know though that you were all safe. You weren't with us in the vision, but Tony had told me that you were all safe." I meet Tony's eyes and see him looking at me inquisitively. I do my best not to think of the details of that particular vision.

"I don't get why my dad was there at the cabin though," Alec speaks up. His eyes are filled with emotions that I can't fully comprehend. I couldn't imagine knowing that someone in my family was playing on the dark side's team. Marya rubs his shoulder in a comforting gesture.

Tony answers Alec, even though it wasn't really a

question. "Blake was in cahoots with Zack. He wanted to get a hold of Willow's powers just as much as Zack did. It would be outlandish for us to presume that he would simply give up hunting Willow just because Zack was removed from the equation."

Alec doesn't look happy about Tony's answer but he doesn't respond either.

"There were a lot of people working with Zack. I'm sure your father isn't the only one leading this mission to hunt me down. There were dozens of other bidders in the room who saw what a single dose of my blood could do," I tell Alec. "I'm so sorry, Alec…about your dad."

This time he does little to hide the emotions running amuck in his navy eyes. "He's not my dad. He's simply the man who fathered me. He ceased being my dad long ago. I really should feel betrayed or hurt or confused at my father's involvement in this mess, but I'm not. I mean, I'm mad as hell, but I can't say that I'm surprised." His eyes turn fierce. He's still staring at me when he says, "I *will* stop him." His determination resonates from his face.

My mouth stays open, but no words come out. What does one say to that? I can't imagine the position that Alec is in right now. I can feel the anger, betrayal, and pain casting off him in waves. His inner-strength and his demand for justice are equally as strong. I have to force myself to close off my empathic abilities.

"We should probably get moving again," my dad intercedes.

We nod our heads and quietly head out again.

After a few more hours of walking, we reach a large clearing more than a hundred yards in length. It isn't until we see the clearing that we realize that the snow is still coming down just as powerfully as before. We were protected for the most part under the covering of the trees.

We use our invisibility as we step out into the clearing. I look from my left to the right and notice it isn't a normal clearing in the woods—it's a road. I wonder where it leads.

The invisibility does little for the trail we are making in the snow though. Tony's been doing his best to cover our tracks, but it isn't perfect. We walk through snow that has accumulated to be over twelve inches, if not more. We have to pick up our feet to walk through it. It seems to take forever before we are back under the covering of the forest again. Being out in the open and exposed in this eerie weather, with more than one party of hunters after us, is nerve wracking.

"We're almost there," my dad whispers.

We keep our invisibility up as we start ascending a large slope.

"This is the safest way. The road back there will take us close to the safe house but I don't want to chance the exposure. We will have to climb a little ways," he tells me.

"No problem," I tell him.

We reach the point that we have to start using our hands to climb. Tony throws Sebastian on this back and says, "Hang on, little man." Sabby giggles as Tony makes a choking sound and says, "Whoa! Not that tight."

The climb isn't hard. The snow for the most part made it a little easier since it packs around where our shoes step in and provides a sort of foothold for us.

Tony offers me his hand when I make it to the top. I accept it and he pulls me swiftly onto flat ground. He takes the opportunity to pull me close into his chest and kiss the bridge of my nose. His lips are cold but the gesture warms me nonetheless.

I smile when I see Connor and Alec helping their girlfriends up the last part too. It's very chivalrous. I suddenly find myself feeling sad for my dad. Or am I feeling the sadness coming from my dad? I'm not sure which. The knots form in my chest as I see the forlorn look on his face. If I miss my mom this much, how much more does the man who loved her with all his heart miss her? What would I do if I lost Tony? I have no idea how my father has kept moving through this.

"Because he loves you and your brother," Tony answers my own personal questions. *"I'm sorry. I know I don't need to listen in on every thought you have. It's hard though. I'm still getting used to these abilities and when I feel you hurting, I have to try to help you."*

I look into his warm, forest-green eyes. *"I know. I'm sorry that I got upset with you earlier. The gift that we have is so special and I took it for granted. I love you."*

"I love you too," Tony says aloud.

"I wuv you too, Wello," Sabby adds.

We both look down at him with grins on our faces. This little boy is the light in all of our darkness. "I love you too, Sabby. I think Daddy needs a hug. What do you think?"

Sabby puts his little finger up to his chin and smiles really big. "I think yes!" He giggles, runs over, and attacks my dad with a bear hug.

My dad grunts but then smiles big. "Be gentle with your old man, Sabby."

"Oh, sawwy." He loosens his grip.

My dad places a kiss on top of his curls.

"We'll take care of him," I whisper to the wind, in case my mom can hear me. I hope she knows that we'll do everything in our power to make sure my dad isn't lonely.

"Are we ready to move?" Alec asks, breaking my thoughts. He's standing there with his arm around a seriously shivering Marya.

"Yes, it's only a little ways from here," my dad says.

He takes the lead and we head diagonally back towards where I assume the road would have led us. We stop and use our invisibility when we get nearby, taking it as a good sign that we can still use our powers. It means that the military isn't nearby. Or at least, that they aren't using whatever device they used to shut our powers down previously.

We stop just within the tree line, which opens to a snow-covered driveway, leading to a large, two-story log cabin. In front of the doorway is an engraved wooden sign, labeling it the Hideaway Bed and Breakfast. The large front porch spans the entire length of its front. Rocking chairs, heavy with the snow that drifted in with the wind, line the porch.

There is no sign of life around the cabin. Inside the windows, no lights glow. I look to my dad. "Do you think they left?" I whisper.

"I don't know. Perhaps." My dad looks confused. "This place was so well hidden though. I'm surprised they would have moved out so soon."

A sinking feeling fills my gut. That, or someone forced them to move out. The memory of the covered trucks carting away Erik's people, Lee, and the others comes flooding back. "We need to check inside."

Without an answer, we step out of the trees and make our way to the cabin door. Tony, Alec, and my dad have their guns out. I pull mine out as well, just in case. The door is sitting partially open. Some snow has made its way into the entryway. Tony takes the lead and opens the door the rest of the way. The first room is filled with large, leather furniture that all faces the huge fireplace with a cobblestone hearth. There are a few cups and plates strung about on the end tables and coffee tables. We walk past them into the formal-dining room. Three long, wooden tables are covered in a disarray of plates half-filled with breakfast foods. I take a closer peek at the food. It's not moldy and there are no flies flying about, so it must be pretty fresh. A few chairs are lying on their backs on the ground.

"What happened in here?" Marya asks, mimicking the question in all of our minds.

Connor doesn't wait for us to clear the rest of the

first floor before he starts calling out, "Lillie! Mom, Dad!" His concern and worry is so thick it envelopes the entire space. Claire stays by his side while he runs from room to room. It's hard to see him like this. Connor is usually so carefree and goofy. I hadn't even thought about his family being here.

Tony and I make our way up the stairs together. I continue to pray that everyone is okay—that everyone is safe. We start searching the individual rooms but come up empty. We pass room after room that was left in utter disarray. There definitely was a struggle in this place, but perhaps not a violent one. Thankfully, we've found no signs of blood and no lifeless bodies.

"Lillie!" Connor yells out as he runs up the stairs. His face is twisted with worry and his breathing is heavy.

Claire looks just as worried. Her eyes dart from Connor to me. She's never seen him like this before either—like he's coming unglued. "It's going to be okay, Connor."

He shakes his head as he searches every inch of this floor. "No, no it's not! She was my responsibility. I'm her brother!"

"Maybe she's with your parents. Maybe they got away," Claire says assuredly. She tries to put her hand on his back but he whirls around to face her.

"Did you see those chairs? The food? These people didn't get away, Claire." His eyes are filling with tears.

My heart nearly splits in two at seeing him so anguished. I focus my empathic abilities on him like I've seen Erik do. I think calm and peaceful thoughts. Soon his body relaxes and his shoulders fall a tad.

Claire, who saw the change, looks over at me. She mouths, "Thank you."

I nod my head. We start looking through the remainder of the rooms. When we've searched the final one, we realize that the place is in fact empty. I look over at Connor, who is at the far end of the hall, and my gut wrenches. Claire pulls him into her arms.

The fear and worry is so thick that I think about turning it off, but don't. For some reason, I feel like I owe it to Connor to feel his emotions with him. The fear is almost overwhelming, to the point that my heart actually speeds up like it would if I were scared. It's almost like he's terrified. Is that a normal emotion in a situation like this? Something feels off about it. "They'll be okay," I call to Connor, attempting to comfort him.

He doesn't answer me and I realize it's because he's crying. Claire is rubbing his back as she holds on to him. I make my way across the hallway towards them and halfway down, the emotions flip. The terrified sensation switches—there is still a note of fear but in a *fear of the unknown* kind of way. Not in a, *my life is in danger* way.

Tony is at my side and when I look into his black eyes, I can see that he felt the change too. We both stare at each other a bit perplexed. I turn around and start walking away from Connor, towards the last room again. The feeling of terror increases the closer and closer I get to the end of the hall.

Tony catches on even before I do. "It's okay. You're

safe. We're not going to hurt you," he calls out to nobody in particular.

I hold my breath as I realize his conclusion. Someone is hiding. Someone is very, very scared and hiding from us. I follow Tony's lead. "It's okay. I promise that you're safe. You can come out and we will take care of you." The feelings change from terror to confusion, to hope and then to mistrust.

Connor and Claire come over to us, wondering who we are calling out to. "Did you find someone?" Connor asks. "Lillie! Did you find Lillie?" he yells out to me.

I shake my head. "No, I just feel like someone is here. They're hiding. They're very, very scared."

"Lillie! Lillie baby, it's me, Connor. If you're here, please come out," he calls frantically.

"Connor, it might not be Lillie. It could be anyone." Tony tries to calm him down using his empathic ability like I did earlier.

Connor fights it all the way and continues to call for Lillie. The sound of a loud thump above us causes us to go quiet. The rest of our group has come up the stairs to see what's happening.

I look up at the ceiling where the thump came from. *There's an attic!* "Someone is up there," I say, pointing upwards.

Connor's expression turns hopeful. With Tony's help, he pulls down the attic door in the ceiling. A built-in ladder descends along with the door. Connor is the first to climb up.

Ending ELE

"Wait, it could be a trap," Alec calls out.

Connor could care less. I hear him step foot into the attic above us.

Tony climbs up behind him and calls down to me. "It's mostly insulation. It's not finished out. Be careful where you step, Connor. Stay on the framing studs."

"Lillie!" Connor calls into the dark attic.

"Co-co?" a shivery little voice calls out.

"Lillie!" Connor yells excitedly, then there is a thud and a yelp. I look up to see Connor's leg sticking through the ceiling.

"I said to stay on the studs," Tony yells up above, slapping his palm against his forehead.

Alec runs to where Connor's foot is sticking through the ceiling and he helps push it back up through the sheetrock. I climb up the stairs halfway so I can see what's going on inside the attic. A small window allows just enough light for me to see Tony helping Connor get back up on the studs.

"Co-Co!" a little girl's voice calls out from the far end of the attic. That's when I see the coppery red hair. She's shaking and sitting on her knees on one of the wooden planks in the far corner of the attic. Another woman is sitting behind her, trying to keep her from running across the sheetrock and falling through the ceiling like her brother did. I look at the woman a little closer, assuming that it would be Connor's mom. It's not though. She is the teacher from the shelter, the one who took care of Sabby and all the other children.

"Lillie!" Connor's voice is filled with relief.

"A-rre the-they g-g--gone?" Ms. Wallobee calls to us. She's shivering from the cold, so much so that it takes a second for us to realize what she's asking. They must not have had enough time to get a coat before fleeing to the attic.

Not sure who she is referring to, both Tony and Connor nod their heads, answering in unison, "Yes."

They make their way across the planks in the attic. Connor grabs Lillie's hand first and turns to guide her safely across the room. Tony helps Ms. Wallobee up. "Careful," I hear him guiding her.

When Connor and Lillie reach the ladder, I hold my arms out to her. She puts her cold arms around me and I help her down. Connor follows her and the second he touches the ground, Lillie turns and bolts into his arms. "I w-wa-was s-ooo sss-carred," she says, shivering and crying.

Claire runs up with two wool blankets. She drapes the first one over Lillie's shoulders and then joins Connor in a group hug.

I take the other blanket from her and give it Ms. Wallobee when she makes it down the stairs. She accepts it gratefully. Her short, dark hair is messy and her glasses are askew over her neon-yellow eyes, but she still manages to look beautiful and very studious. I notice now that she's about my mother's age. I can tell by the look in her eye that she remembers me.

"Ms. W!" Sebastian comes running over to her. He throws his arms around her legs.

"Sss-ebbastian." It's all she says because her teeth are chattering, making it too hard to talk. I can see the happiness in her eyes at seeing my little brother again. She hugs him tightly and then runs her hand over his curls. It takes a few minutes for her to warm up enough to talk coherently. My little brother stays close to her side the entire time. He tries to rub her arm to help her warm up. I can feel the love that she has for him and Lillie emanating from her. She loves children and considers her students as her own.

Her face turns sad after those feelings run their course. "I could only save Lillie. She was the closest to me." Ms. Wallobee's shivering voice is filled with emotion.

"Did you see who came?" my dad asks her.

"No. I could hear a muffled voice on a loud speaker. Then all of a sudden, everyone's eye colors started going back to normal. Most everyone who was upstairs with me ran downstairs to see what the commotion was about. I was about to be behind them but wanted to grab my jacket first. That's when I heard the screaming and things crashing around downstairs. I saw Lillie coming out of the bathroom and grabbed her. The attic was the first place I thought to go since my sister and I used to hide in our attic when I was younger. They didn't even look for us up there."

"It sounds like the same military people," Tony says.

"Do you know what they want? Why did they take everyone?" Ms. Wallobee asks.

"We don't know yet. We were hoping to come and meet up with your group, to warn you first. I guess we didn't make it in time. They had taken the people I was staying with too. Lee was there and was taken as well. I'm sorry, Ms. Wallobee," I tell her.

She shakes her head. "It's not your fault, Willow. And you can call me Carrie."

I smile sadly at her. I still can't help but feel like we were too late to be of help. "Thank you, Carrie. Do you know when they came? How long were you in the attic?" I ask.

"It was only this morning that they came," she tells me.

"We'll get everyone back," my dad tells her.

She nods her head and says, "Thank you, Henry."

"We should move out just in case they send someone back over here to do a second sweep," Tony says.

"Yes, I agree," my dad concurs.

Carrie grabs her coat and a few items, while Connor helps Lillie get dressed for the cold air outside. We search the place for their usual weapons storage area, but we come up short. I guess whoever took them confiscated the weapons as well.

"Where should we go from here?" I question since I'm not familiar with this area.

Tony thinks about it. "I'm not sure. I know we shouldn't stray too far. We need to be able to help the others so that means we have to be close enough to scout out the area."

"There's a river not too far from here. I'm sure that we would be able to find some houses or cabins along the bank. This area was a premier vacation spot back before the virus," Carrie says.

"Which way is the river?" my dad asks her.

"I can't say I'm completely positive, but if I were to guess, I'd say to the north," she answers while she wraps a scarf around her neck.

"Let's do this then," I say. Tony gives me a silly grin at my enthusiasm.

While I dread going back out in this winter wonderland, I still can't help but feel safer the further we get from the safe house—which is no longer considered safe. I don't doubt that the soldiers will come back to check for any returnees. The strange part of that is that I don't necessarily find myself as fearful of running into them as I am of running into Blake and his posse. The soldiers came in and hauled everyone away, but we didn't see any casualties from the takeover. Blake and his group of mad men were ready for a hostile takeover. If my dad's vision was accurate, my friends and family wouldn't have fared so well.

We pass a few houses and cabins along our journey north but decide that they are too close to the other safe house for comfort. We continue in search of this river that Carrie told us about, travelling for a few hours through the woods. My legs are starting to ache from having to march through the snow.

Tony, having sensed my discomfort, picks me up in his arms. I laugh as he spins me around once and then continues walking with the others while keeping me in his arms.

"I'm perfectly capable of walking," I say with a huge grin.

"I know and I am perfectly capable of carrying you for miles." He leans in and kisses me on my cold nose.

I snuggle in closer to him as he carries me. I happen to catch my dad looking at us. First, I see a small hint of a smile and when he sees me looking, he shakes his head and rolls his eyes. I laugh to myself. My dad's not too keen on my being in a relationship, but he also likes to see me happy.

Soon Sabby convinces me that he needs me to give him a piggyback ride. So Tony reluctantly sets me back down on the white earth and Sabby climbs aboard. He rides on my back for what seems like hours, but I'm sure it was just thirty frustrating minutes. Each house we come to seems more unsafe than the last and we still haven't reached the river. All the trees that would normally surround each house have been cleared, giving anyone walking nearby a perfect view. The sun is beginning to set, while the wind is turning colder and becoming stronger, whipping my hair wildly. Sebastian begins to bury his face behind me to keep from getting frostbite on his little nose.

A soft rumbling sound caresses my ears. I scrunch my eyebrows, and then Tony's eyes meet mine. He can hear the sound too.

"Is that rain?" I question aloud. By this time, everyone that's with us can hear it as well. The trees become more and more dense again and the rumbling sound gets louder and more distinguishable. "I know that sound. I just can't place it," I say under my breath.

Tony nods his head and looks around us. We trudge through the snow one step at a time. It is almost to our knees at this point, making it very difficult, if not impossible, to walk. Instead, we end up wading through it, making long, streak-like patterns in it.

It's nearly impossible to see more than a few feet in front of us because of the thick sheets of white falling down from the sky. I can barely even see my dad and Connor, who have taken the lead of our pack. The sound continues to get louder and louder until it's almost deafening.

I can feel a strange emotion rolling off Tony and when I look over at him, a stark realization dawns on his face. "Stop!" he yells as loud as he can. He starts running towards the front of our group because the noise is so loud. "Stop!" I am on his heels when he reaches my dad and Connor a second later. He grabs them both by the shoulder at the same time and brings them to a halt.

Startled, Connor says, "What the…?"

"Stay back!" Tony interrupts his questioning.

We're all a bit confused by the intense seriousness that Tony is projecting, but everyone quiets down and stands still.

Satisfied that he has our attention, he motions for us to follow him. We trail Tony as he inches forward, only a few steps ahead, moving very cautiously. I can vaguely make out a break in the trees, although the visibility is very limited. My feet are cold as ice and I feel my legs going numb as well. The rushing and roaring sound is so loud now that I can barely even hear my thoughts.

Tony stops abruptly again and holds out his arms on either side of him. He turns his head to look at us. "Stop," he commands and, even though we can't hear him, we can read his lips.

I read his thoughts even before I see what is causing the noise. Tony mouths the word, "Careful," to us, and then he allows us to inch closer so we can see what he's looking at.

The wind carries the snow away from my face for just a moment, but it's all I need in order to see the sheer cliff that stands before us. Running off the adjacent cliff is a massive waterfall that jets down to the churning waters below. I suck in my breath at the sight before the snow takes it away from me again. If it hadn't have been for Tony, someone may have died. The thought is unsettling. We were trucking through the forest pretty quickly and the snowfall might not have allowed us to see what was only a few steps ahead of us.

Everyone takes a turn looking over the cliff and gawking at the majesty of the entire situation. "Well," says Connor loudly, "I guess we found the river."

FOUR

I snort. That's the understatement of the century.

Claire punches Connor in the arm playfully, and then puts her gloved hands back under her arms to keep warm.

"That's great that we found the river, but we really need to find shelter," I say, stating the obvious. We try looking around us but all we see is white, white, and more white, for as far as the eyes can see…oh, and a river.

"Look," Ms. Wallobee states as she points below her feet. We all squint and stare, trying to see what she points at. The snow shifts again and for a brief second, I see the opening of a small cave along the cliff wall. It's not easily accessible but there are a few small ledges that lead down to the cave, making it somewhat manageable to get to.

With no other immediately better option available, we decide to go for it. Tony takes the lead, checking his stepping on the way down. With all the snow that's piled around us, it makes it almost impossible to tell where to take our next step. We all grab hands as if we were in a long train and place our feet exactly where the person in front of us placed theirs.

For a moment, I watch in horror as Tony loses his footing up ahead. I hold my breath, unable to scream as I watch my father grip his arm and pull him back up. My heart pounds in my chest and I hold onto Sebastian's hand a little more tightly. I take a few deep breaths to reassure myself that Tony's okay.

It takes us a good half hour to make our way down to the mouth of the cave. When we all reach solid ground, we huddle around each other for warmth. Tony digs in the snow and finds a large rock. He throws it into the cave to make sure it's unoccupied. We hear it ricochet off the cave walls. A few grey bats fly out for a moment but fly right back in when the snow hits their wings.

I shiver, but not because of the cold. The only thing I can think about is the vampire-like bats I saw on my tablet when I was younger. I remember having nightmares for weeks after I read about those. Tony motions for us all to enter but remains cautious. The mouth of the cave is only large enough for one person at a time. It's amazing that Ms. Wallobee was even able to see it. It's almost completely covered by large boulders.

When it's my turn to go into the cave, I have to take a deep breath and mentally put my big-girl panties on. It's pitch black and there's no telling how many bats and other animals we're sharing this cave with. Claire, who's in front of me, stops. We wait a few seconds, hear the click of a flashlight, and, at once, the cave is illuminated. The light bounces off the cave walls, revealing the slick, rocky surface. The light hits the ceiling for only a moment and I catch a glimpse of a few bats giving their wings a territorial flap. Sebastian's grip tightens on my hand and I try to give him a comforting squeeze. Tony spends a few more minutes checking out the area. It seems the cave is only about twenty-feet deep and about fifteen feet in height. The ceiling was far too low for my comfort zone, especially with the bats involved.

I look over at Claire, who seems excited to see the bats. She stares up at them in wonder. "Bats don't usually pick caves like this to hibernate in. Usually, they pick between only a few large caves in this part of the US to spend the winter. Those caves have a certain type of airflow that helps stabilize the cave and protect them against a freeze. If I were to guess, since there are less than twenty bats here, I would say that these poor guys tried to outfly the quick change of temperature." She looks back down and her eyes meet mine. Her face turns sad. "I doubt all these little guys will survive this freeze. They don't fare well at all when the temperature drops below thirty-five."

In that moment, the fear I had over spending the night with the bats is replaced with empathy for their situation. Like us, their lives and their routines were thrown off-kilter. Their worlds flipped on their axis. Much like us survivors, they are just trying to live another day in this crazy life, never knowing if today will be their last. My heart hurts for them. My heart hurts for everyone who has had to endure the turbulence of these times, including us.

As if sensing my forlorn emotions, Tony takes my hand and leads me further into the cave. The newfound silence engulfs my ears as the heavy snow and waterfall is muffled behind us. Setting our belongings down in a heap, we collapse in exhaustion. We count our blessings when Tony finds a few pieces of firewood that must have been left by a camper, who knows how long ago. He starts a fire nearer to the mouth of the cave and we all scoot closer to warm our hands and feet.

The heat is exquisite and I move closer to take as much of it as I can, until my feet tingle from the warmth of the fire, making me uncomfortable. I heal them in a few minutes and continue to revel in the warmth.

The fire crackles, filling the cave with an eerie whisper. Shadows dance across the walls from the small movements we make. Every now and then, you can hear a bat flap its wings as it flies from one place to another. There's a constant dripping sound in the far corner.

My dad pulls out a couple cans of…and that's when I realize there are no labels on them. I scrunch my eyebrows. "What is it?" I ask, breaking the deafening silence.

A small, mischievous smile splays on Tony's lips and he shrugs his shoulders. He gets a playful gleam in his eye and it's all I can do to keep from laughing.

"What's so funny?" I question him once more, still studying the cans.

He smiles at me and answers. "Well, living out in the middle of nowhere, we sort of ran out of things to do when I was younger. So, one day I thought it would be fun to remove all the labels off the cans." I scoff.

"But, why would you do that?" I question,

Ending ELE

interrupting him. "Then you don't know what you're going to eat."

His smile gets wider. "Exactly!" he says to me.

I furrow my brow further but keep the playfulness on my lips.

"So, my parents and I would play dinner roulette. In other words, you get what you get and you don't throw a fit."

I shake my head and laugh. "Of course you did."

So, against my better judgment, and because I have absolutely no choice, I grab a random can, hoping it's not something like tuna fish.

Sebastian, on the other hand, looks at the cans like Christmas has come early. His little fingers hover over each one, wiggling like he's going to take the can before he moves onto the next one, and the next. Finally, he picks one up and giggles with glee. I guess I can see where a kid might think this is fun. Especially if they're adventurous eaters like Sebastian is.

With his precious can in tow, Sabby comes and sits down next to me. "I wonder what I get!" he exclaims with excitement. Then a thought comes raining down on his parade and he looks at me worriedly. "I hope it not peas!"

I laugh. "Yeah, hopefully there are no alien eggs for you."

"How about this champ, if you get peas, I'll trade you," Tony tells my little brother.

Sabby's face lights up and he says, "Deal!"

"You just made a friend for life," my dad says to

Tony. They share a smile and an understanding look that warms me. I didn't realize how important it was to me that my dad approves of Tony. I notice in that small exchange that he does.

Thankfully, with all the rush that went on earlier, Tony remembered to pack a can opener. We take turns passing it around, each peering into our own mystery meal with guarded anticipation.

"Score!" Alec says when he unveils his pork and beans. Marya, Ms. Wallobee, and Claire all end up with some kind of stew. Sebastian gets chicken noodle soup and he's more than thrilled.

Connor jiggles the can opener and pops his open. He places the open container next to the fire to get a better look and his face goes white. "Please tell me you're kidding…" he says, lost in thought.

"Hey," I intervene. "How bad could it possibly be?"

Connor looks at me like I'm growing a second head. "Pickled Beets?" he questions, smelling the contents.

Well, he has a good point. I'm not sure why they make those either. I shrug my shoulders with a laugh and watch as Connor struggles to eat his dinner. The faces he makes are priceless and when there's no entertainment to be had, well, Connor's all we got.

Claire laughs at her boyfriend. She gives him a peck on the cheek and then happily shares her stew with the man she loves.

Lillie tells him, "I will share too, Co-co." She holds up a spoonful of Spaghetti-Os for her brother to take a bite.

He offers a bite of his in return. Lillie scrunches up her freckled, little nose and shakes her head.

"Yeah, Co-Co. Nobody wants your beets," Alec jabs at him.

Connor turns and glares. He points his spoon filled with the nasty red vegetables at him. "Only Lillie gets to call me that."

Alec throws his hands in the air in mock surrender and Lillie giggles at the two of them.

I finally get passed the royal can opener and discover some kind of hot dog things, only much smaller. I heat them up over the fire and pop one in my mouth. "Eh, not the worst I've eaten," I say.

My dad winds up with a simple can of green beans and Tony gets salmon.

"How did you end up with the prized can of Salmon?" I ask in mock disdain.

A snarky smile inches its way up his lips. He turns to me and whispers in my ear, "Practice makes perfect. Don't you think I've learned a thing or two about how my favorite cans look?" His breath on my ear tickles.

"Cheater," I say, playfully punching his shoulder. He steals a kiss on my cheek and then gives me a bite.

Lillie, Sebastian, and Ms. Wallobee, I mean Carrie, sit together near the corner of the cave. They're all three lying on their backs as Carrie makes shadow puppets with her hands on the cave wall. I watch as both kids' eyes get heavy and they settle in for the night.

Everyone else is paired off: Connor and Claire,

Alec and Marya, Tony and me…then there's my dad. The ol' third wheel. I feel bad as I watch him try to cope by himself, all alone. I pat Tony's leg with my hand and get up to go sit with my dad.

"How's it going, old man?" I tease.

He gives me a smile but I can see the effort behind it. He sighs and I sit next to him, placing my head on his shoulder. His arms instinctively wrap around me in a comforting hug.

"I miss her too…" I tell him.

His scratchy stubble rubs against my head as he nods in affirmation. "You remind me so much of her," he says simply. "It lets me miss her just a little bit less when you're around."

Hearing him say this makes me smile. I loosen from his embrace and look up at my dad. "Thanks, Dad. That means a lot." He gives my shoulders a squeeze.

Tony gets up and comes to joins us. "Hi, Mr. Mosby," he says to my dad.

"Tony, I think by now we're on a first name basis. Please, call me Henry." Tony nods his head and sits down next to us. "Yes, sir."

I stifle a laugh at Tony being proper. The Tony I've come to know is the sarcastic, playful, badgering, yet loving Tony. It sounds funny when he talks that way. "Salmon?" He offers the can to my dad.

My dad raises one eyebrow. "How did you score salmon? All I got was green beans." He takes his fork and jabs it into Tony's can.

"Practice makes perfect," Tony answers.

"Cheater." My dad copies my response, which gains a chuckle from Tony. My dad places the small offering in his mouth, savoring the taste. "Thanks," he says after he finishes chewing.

Tony nods his head and then finishes off the last of the salmon.

After we finish eating, we lean back against the rock structures behind us.

"Remember the time Mom tried to cook Thanksgiving dinner?" I say out loud.

Dad lets out a deep, belly-jiggling laugh, almost choking on his food. "Oh yes, that was an…interesting Thanksgiving! We ended up ordering in pizza that night. That is, after we got all the smoke out and sent the fire department home."

Tony smiles with us. "So, I'm guessing Alice wasn't the best cook?" he asks.

My dad and I nod enthusiastically. "That's an understatement," I tell him. Our smiles return to remembrance as we all recall my mom.

"Remember that time she lost the ornament boxes for the Christmas tree?" My dad asks.

I giggle, remembering that year. "Oh yes!" I say. "The yearlong Christmas, couldn't ever forget that!" Tony gives a chuckle. I tell him the story. "We had to leave our Christmas tree up all year because my mom wouldn't let us put it away without those boxes. She was scared the ornaments would break if we took it down without them. I remember having people over a few times that summer. We tried to explain it, but they never quite understood."

My dad interjects, "And remember how it sat in the front window and it was connected to the front room light? Every time we turned the light on, the Christmas tree would light up too. Our neighbors would just shake their heads at us every time they walked by."

"Oh, I got one," I say. "Remember that time she put liquid dish soap in the dishwasher? She filled the entire soap container with it." I laugh, a good, hearty laugh.

"Yeah," my dad continues, "then we went out and ran our errands. When we returned, even before we got inside, there were bubbles coming out the front door."

Tony begins laughing with us too. My dad's laughing so hard, he can hardly speak. "The look on the faces of the water restoration people was priceless! Alice kept repeating over and over again to them that the label said *dish* soap. They just looked at her like she'd lost her mind."

We laugh and laugh, remembering those precious moments. We laugh until it hurts and then laugh some more. Finally, the laughter dies down and is replaced with silence and memory. I miss her so much it hurts. I hurt for my dad and the fact that he no longer has her either. I hurt because Sebastian was so young when we lost her and he never had the chance to really get to know her like I did.

Tony puts his arm around me and I lean into him. "*I miss her,*" I tell Tony in secret.

A muted silence follows and then Tony tells me, "*I*

know you do. I miss her too."

The fire is beginning to die down and the cave is filled with the sound of crackling embers and echoing drips. Alec grabs a few more twigs that he finds and tosses them into the flames. We all lay in a circle around the fire with our heads either rested on each other or on our packs.

My body is exhausted but my mind is racing and I can't seem to shut it off. I'm getting the same vibe from Tony as well. I sit up and see him eyeing me in the dim light. I grab his hand and lead him to the mouth of the cave in an alcove surrounded by boulders. We find a few large rocks to sit on next to each other and watch the snow fall in sheets until it meets the waterfall below. The sound of the waterfall is soothing, yet scary. So much power in one area.

"I'm worried," I tell Tony while watching the snow. Silence makes its way between us as we sit huddled together to keep warm.

"Me too," Tony answers simply.

Words don't need to be shared right now. We just give the other person the room to worry. Sometimes you just need to let your mind race so it'll tire and slow.

After a few minutes in silence, Tony takes my hand in his and kisses me on top of my head. I look up at him, into his eyes. The cacophony around us disappears and it's just him and me. He closes his eyes as I do mine and he leans in to kiss me. Our warm lips meet and I melt into him. He kisses me softly, slowly—his grip firm, yet gentle. He places his hand on the small of my back and pulls me closer. So near that we are both pressed up against the wall of the cave. I reach my hands behind his head and pull him even nearer still. My desires and my morals fight viciously in my head. My desires saying more, more and my morals saying wait, wait. I want so badly to give into my desires, to go further than I should. I can tell by Tony's breathing he desires me in that way too.

Instead of me pulling away, he pulls away first. The connection is broken immediately, like water poured over a roaring fire. I catch my breath as the cool air circles between us. We both breathe heavily only a few inches apart, watching our breath cloud up around us.

Tony pulls back, sitting up straight across from me, his muscles straining against his shirt. Something is wrong—really wrong. I can't tell what color his eyes are or what's going on for that matter, because of the absence of light. "Tony?" I whisper. I shake him but he stays rigid. "Tony?" I say a little more loudly, but remaining quiet, so not to wake the others. After a few more seconds of shaking him, his body goes limp and he sucks in a lungful of air. I waste no time trying to figure out what happened. "Tony, are you okay? Tony?"

His arms encircle me and I hug him back, but pull away almost immediately.

"What's wrong? What was that?" I ask him.

He takes a few more deep breaths and then answers me. "A cabin, I saw a cabin hidden in the woods."

Relief washes over me. "You had a vision?" I ask, even though I know the answer.

Ending ELE

I see his head nod in the shadows. "I'm sorry. I've just never had a vision before. It caught me off guard."

I rub his arms in comfort, willing him to go on. "What else did you see?" I inquire.

He swallows and then says, "I saw this cabin in the woods, not far from here. It was very excluded. I almost didn't realize what it was until the vision pulled me inside. It's huge and has running water and gas. The trees and brush are so overgrown around the entrance that it hides the place well. It's fully stocked, unlike most of the places we've run into." His voice sounds excited, but there's a hint of worry in it.

"That's great, Tony, so how do we get there?" I prod.

Tony takes a deep breath and lets it out rather loudly. "That's the problem. It's on the other side of the waterfall."

I wake in the morning with a crick in my back.

Sleeping on the hard floor of the cave doesn't make for a restful sleep. I figure that I'm the first one up until I notice Tony is nowhere around me.

Honestly, I don't even remember falling asleep last night. I get to my feet and look over all the sleeping bodies. I can't help but laugh at Connor, who sleeps in the fetal position. With him being so tall, it's kind of awkward.

On a serious note, Tony isn't among the sleeping bodies. I tiptoe away from the others to look for him. The cave isn't that big and it doesn't take long for me to discover that he's sitting outside the mouth of the cave with a pair of binoculars in his hand.

I walk quietly up behind him and wrap my arms around his middle. "Couldn't sleep?" I ask in a husky voice. I clear my throat.

He sets the binoculars down at his side and pulls me into his arms.

I can't help but notice his eyes look tired and drawn. "Did you sleep at all?" I ask.

He gives me a small smirk and shakes his head.

"That vision I got last night kept me up thinking. I couldn't get my mind to turn off. I was out here at first light with my binoculars to scope out the area. The snow began to let up around two this morning."

I rub his back, knowing what lack of sleep can do to a person.

"Here, take these." He hands me the binoculars and moves around until he's behind me. I put the binoculars to my eyes and scan the horizon. He helps me move the binoculars in place and I look at where he points. "Do you see that? It's not much but I think that's where the house is. It matches my vision."

I squint my eyes really hard to try to see it, but come up empty. Ignoring my lack of vision, I nod my head that I saw it anyway. No sense in discouraging him even more when he hasn't even had a lick of sleep.

Tony begins pacing in front of me. "The problem lies with how on earth we get there. Crossing the freezing water isn't an option. Even if we hike down to the bottom, there isn't a bridge that I can see anywhere along this river that could get us across." He stops pacing and looks me dead on. "*This* is what has kept me up all night. It drives me crazy that I can't come up with some semblance of an idea about what to do…not even a sliver." He pursues his lips and then turns his attention back out of the cave in the direction of the house.

He looks so tired and exhausted. Protective instincts start taking over at seeing him like this. He needs to rest or at least eat something. I hear the others stirring behind us.

"Come on, let's get some mystery breakfast. But, promise me you'll give me the hook up this time." I manage to get a small smile from him as I take his hand and lead us back to the others.

The fire has been fed with new wood that I assume Tony must have brought in from his night-owl interlude. I look over at Connor, who sits next to it with a stack of cans. He's shaking them and putting them up to his ear. He even tried to smell one of them.

Claire sits a few feet away, smiling at him adoringly.

Tony leans into my ear. "Watch this," he says facetiously.

I stifle a grin as Tony makes his way over to Connor. Connor watches him intently as Tony grabs a can of food and picks up the can opener.

"Wait just a second!" Connor says passionately, pointing his finger at Tony. "I got pickled beets for dinner last night and I don't plan on repeating that. I'll take that," he says as he snatches the can out of Tony's hand.

Tony seems like he's upset but I can tell this is all just an act. Connor grins like the Cheshire cat and grabs the can opener from Tony as well. He sets the can on the open fire to heat up. Tony bends down and picks up two more cans. I'm assuming he just grabbed me breakfast as well. He places them over the fire and comes sits next to me.

"Wait for it," Tony says in a mild whisper. I bite the inside of my cheeks to keep from smiling too much and giving it all away. A few minutes later, Connor stumbles to get the can out of the fire with the help of a stick he found in the cave. He uses his shirt to hold the hot can as he wrestles with the can opener.

I put my hand over my mouth because I just know I'm going to be laughing out loud in a few moments. Tony never fails to impress me with his wicked ways.

Lo and behold, Connor pops the lid off his can. The smell begins to permeate the entire cave as he holds a flashlight over the top of the can. He immediately puts his hand over his face and nose, trying to contain a dry heave. He stands up, throws his hands on hips, and finds Tony with his eyes. "You CANNOT tell me that you had a hankering for sauerkraut this morning!"

I can't contain my laughter anymore. Connor plays the part of a pranked victim perfectly.

Tony holds his hands up in the air. "What can I say? Gotta love sauerkraut at seven in the morning."

Connor isn't buying this. "Well played, my man, well played." He puts his first two fingers up to his eyes and turns them towards Tony's eyes. "I'll be watching you…" He pauses for dramatic effect. "And just when you think you've won, BAM. That's right, you'll get yours." Connor keeps his eyes narrowed playfully on Tony's.

"Game on," Tony retorts as he gives his head a slight nod.

"Men," both Claire and I say at the same time. We share a sideways smile and shake our heads. We watch as Connor pokes at his meal with a fork. He holds his nose and pops a strand of sauerkraut into his mouth. He gags as he attempts to swallow the delectable morsel.

"Hey," I say, trying to lend a hand. He turns his attention to me, contorted face and all. "If you squeeze your left thumb, it will stop your gag reflex."

The blank look he gives me is epic.

"Seriously, just try it." He narrows his eyes at me, assessing if I'm telling him the truth or if I've crossed to the dark side with Tony and his pranks. He purses his lips and attempts bite number two with his thumb firmly held tight. He bites down on the sauerkraut and begins chewing. Swallowing, he glances over at me.

"I can't tell if this works because you're psyching me out or because I'm holding my thumb. But seriously… thanks."

I shoot him a grin. "No prob."

Tony fills everyone in on his vision last night. He takes the others to the same spot and tries to show them the house he sees in the distance. Shockingly, no one else is able to see what he's talking about. Every time they say they can't see it, he points back to me and says, "Well Willow can! What's wrong with you people?"

I feel my face getting red, so I busy myself with packing up our supplies. Even when all the work is done, I find something else to rearrange. Tony stays up at the mouth of the cave, convincing the others about the location of the cabin.

"So, what's the plan, Willow?" Claire asks me.

I jump a little because I didn't hear her sneak up on me. I put my hand over my heart. "Sorry, Claire Bear,"

I laugh. "I was off in my own world and didn't hear you coming."

She shares a smile with me. "Sorry."

I attempt to answer her original question. Taking a deep breath, I let it out. "To be honest, I haven't come up with one yet. The only thing I can think of right now is that we need to get off this cliff and onto sturdy ground. Once we are back on a flat plane, perhaps it will give us a different vantage point and hopefully an idea about how to proceed." I shrug my shoulders, hoping that was a good enough plan. It has to be because it's all I have.

Claire ponders it for a moment and then nods her head. "I don't see why that won't work."

I finish 'packing' while Claire goes back to the others and reiterates my plan…My lousy plan that obviously won't get us any closer to where we need to be.

We all grab our packs and make sure the fire is completely out. It's stopped snowing for the most part outside. The accumulation still makes our path treacherous, but at least our vision isn't totally obstructed. Holding hands and forming a train, we slowly make our way up the same path we came down the night before.

The bright snow burns my eyes as the sun ricochets off its surface. I can't hold my hand over my eyes because I have to hold onto the person in front of me and the person behind me. I feel like I walk almost blindly up the side of the cliff. It's a little nerve wracking to say the least. After twenty minutes or so and some heavy climbing, we eventually all make it to the top in one piece.

We lean against a few trees and catch our breath. I scan the area, hoping to have some kind of epiphany as to how to cross the waterfall. I look down at the pool of water beneath the falls. There are several fallen trees here and there strung out along the bank of the river. "We could move those and create a bridge to cross the river, if we could just get to the bottom."

Marya notices the fallen trees that I'm looking at. "Yeah, I could totally move those. I just don't see a way down from up here though."

"We could try just walking along this route for a while and hope that the terrain slowly travels downhill," Alec thinks aloud.

Carrie steps in between us to get a better look of the area. "If this is Chikawan Falls, which it looks like it is, we would be travelling quite a ways before we find an easy way down to the river. Even then, we would have eventually had to get wet to get back to this point. I had no idea we were this far north. This waterfall and the cliffs that surround it are famous for being a rock climber's paradise. With such exclusive access to only those who took on the thrill of the climb, people would come from all over the country to rappel down the side of these cliffs and swim in the pools of water at the bottom below."

"Nice…" Connor says. "But how do *we* get down?"

"Man," I say. "If only we could all just jump down into that pool of water."

Connor looks like he is actually thinking that could be a possibility…until Claire sets him straight with a stern look.

Alec pulls a long rope from his pack and holds it up for us to see. "Rappelling anyone?"

At this point, I'm not sure which way is up and which way is down. The color drains from my face and I have to hold onto the tree to remain upright.

I feel Tony's arm wrap securely around my middle. "You okay?" he asks in my ear.

I shake my head from side to side. "No way. There's *no* way I'm rappelling down the side of that cliff," I say, because really, it is *not* an option.

"Well, what do we have here?" Connor says playfully. "We finally find the chink in Willow's armor."

I glare at Connor. "What, are you seriously willing to put your life in the hands of a single rope?"

He gives me a smirk but doesn't reply.

My dad looks around us. "Willow, honey, if we have any chance of getting down there," he points down to the bottom of the waterfall, "then it seems as if it's our only option. I'm not a fan of heights either, but it just doesn't seem like we have a lot of options here."

"Don't get me wrong," I interject. "I'm not scared of heights, you guys. What I'm scared of is dangling from a rope down the side of a cliff! Does that seriously not freak anyone else out?" I ask in bewilderment.

Tony takes me by the arms and forces me to look straight into his face. "Look at me, Willow…really look at me." I calm myself as much as I can and give Tony my full attention. "If I didn't feel it was safe, I would *never* allow you to do this. Not ever." Then his voice turns to a whisper so that only I can hear. "I plan on spending the rest of my life with you. Nothing will stop that." He looks at me with such certainty and love that I melt, completely forgetting my argument. If Tony is as sure about this as he is, then who am I to question him?

I give it a moment more before I speak. "Okay… I'll do it, but only if you're on the other end of that rope."

Tony places his hand on my cheek. "Where else would I be?"

With that, I kiss him softly on the lips.

"Ewww, Wello! That icky!" Sebastian interjects.

I laugh beneath the kiss and break away. Then I make a kissy face and run after Sabby, making smooching noises with my mouth. He giggles and his little head bobs above the powdery snow as he runs away from me. I catch up to him and cover him with kisses. He squeals with delight and I catch sight of my dad smiling back at us in my peripheral vision.

Against my better judgment, I find myself dangling from a rope off the side of the cliff. "Don't look down, don't look down," I mutter over and over again under my breath. The men rigged some kind of rope/pulley contraption and Tony is slowly lowering me down.

The others are already at the bottom of the cliff and they're cheering me on. "You're doing great," I hear Claire and Marya yell from below.

"Wait-a-go, Wello!" Sabby yells at me. Lillie cheers

for me too.

I feel the rope give a little at a time. Tony promised me that he would go as slow as possible. Suddenly, there's a gasp from below; I can tell it's from my father. I make the mistake of looking down and all the blood rushes from my face.

"Tony!" My father yells past me; his voice is on the edge of terror.

I panic, unsure of the problem, but there's nothing I can do. I'm stuck, dangling in midair at least fifty feet above the ground.

"Willow, look up at me." I see Tony peering down at me from the top of the cliff. "I'm going to swing you towards the cliff. There's a ledge you need to grab onto."

Wait, what? I think to myself. *No, this wasn't the plan. Everyone else got down this way—why can't I?* Then I feel a strange sensation in my fingers and look back up. I can see parts of the rope fraying apart along the edge of the cliff. I fight the nausea that is overpowering my thoughts. A fall from this distance could be a death sentence. I don't have time to think. I just act.

The next few seconds go by in a blur as Tony uses all of his strength to swing the rope towards the cliff. I reach my hand out towards the rocky surface above the ledge but I miss it by three or four feet and go swinging back the opposite way again. I watch as more strands of the rope break away. He swings the rope again and the tips of my toes touch the icy snow on the ledge, sending small rocks and pebbles down to my grave. My heart is beating double time when the rope breaks a little more and I drop an inch.

Screams and cries sound out below me. True fear bubbles up within me. I look up and can see in Tony's eyes that there isn't going to be another chance. With a grunt, he swings the rope one final time. I use my legs to push myself along the cliff wall in hopes that our momentum together will bring me to the ledge. As I come upon it, I reach my hand upwards, brace my feet to land, and this time I make contact. I grip my fingernails into the ice and rocks above me as the rope gives a final crack and breaks. I let it fall out of my hands and I force my body to become one with the cliff wall. Small rocks and bits of snow fall down on my face and into my eyes as my fingers continue to search for a firmer grip. I finally clue into the screams of my friends and family below and their new cries of relief. The relief is short-lived as a new problem is presented. Bile forms in my throat as I realize the predicament I'm in. *Now what?* I think to myself in panic. I certainly can't climb my way down. I can't stay on this ledge for long either. It's taking every muscle in my body to stay upright on this small foothold. Why oh why, did Dr. Hasting's not think to invent the gift of flight? That would have been extremely useful right about now.

Tony shouts down from above. "Don't move and hold on tight. I'm on my way." *Thank you, Captain Obvious,* I think to myself as sweat accumulates on my brow.

At first, I'm relieved...my hero is coming to get me once again. But when I see Tony flipping his legs over the side with no rope in sight, I begin to panic. "Tony," I yell. "You cannot free climb down the side of this cliff!"

He pays no heed to my desperate plea and it's all I can do to keep from falling myself. I watch helplessly as he climbs down towards me, losing his footing every third step or so. My stomach is in knots and I feel like I'm going to hurl. I grip onto this ledge for dear life, realizing that if the rocky ledge gives way, then I would be a goner too. I hide my face in the side of the cliff and take deep breaths. I can't watch Tony; he's making me extremely ill at ease.

The silence that once drifted from below is replaced with encouraging words as Tony, I'm guessing, makes his way towards me. I keep my head buried in the rock, not able to look away.

After what seems like millennia, but is probably only five minutes or so, I hear Tony a few feet from me. He reaches his foot out and steps on this tiny ledge with me. "Willow," he says to me.

"Yes," I squeak, still not able to look up.

"I want you to climb on my back," he says.

This gets my blood pumping even more than before. "Climb on your back—are you nuts? That's a death sentence for both of us!"

"Willow," he says, still as calm as ever. "I'm very strong, as are you. I just need for you to climb on my back, hold on tight, and don't move. If you can do that, I can get us both down safely."

I scoff, but really, what other options is there. Call 9-1-1? For the first time since I began dangling from this ledge I look out and into Tony's eyes. They are as calm as ever, steadfast even with their neon-green color.

He whispers in my ear, "Trust me, you and me, we are not done yet. I will get you down."

His breath on my neck sends a tingling sensation through me. *Now is not the time to get all hot and bothered, Willow*, I tell myself.

Tony chuckles, apparently having heard my thoughts.

"Shouldn't you be focusing on your other powers, mister?" I playfully scold him before I take a deep breath and begin climbing onto his back. I wrap my legs around his middle and squeeze like my life depends on it…which sadly, it does. Then we begin to make the journey down to solid ground.

Every time his footing slips, I take a sharp intake of breath and squeeze a little tighter. A rock that Tony grabs ahold of comes loose above our heads. His hand slips and I feel us start to fall but miraculously we stay on course. Through my grip around his neck, I can feel Tony's pulse pounding and adrenaline pumping. "I love you, Tony," I whisper to him. "No matter what."

When we finally land on solid ground, I have a hard time letting him go. He's like my safe haven…and even though I know the danger is over, I just can't make myself let go. My muscles are trembling and so are Tony's. Both of us are visibly shaking in our boots.

My dad comes running over to us and wraps his arms around us both. He stays like that for what seems like hours, when in reality, it's only minutes. I can't even fathom what he felt watching us dangle from the side of that cliff. He emanates feelings of helplessness and relief as we embrace.

He finally pulls away and I'm able to slide down Tony's back, grateful when my feet touch the ground.

My dad looks into Tony's eyes and says, "Tony, my son. Thank you. From the bottom of my heart, thank you. I owe you—everything," he says as if at loss for the right words.

I look over at Tony and can see him blushing as he looks down at the ground. "I would do it again in a heartbeat, sir." Then he turns to look at someone behind me. "But I owe a huge thank you to Marya."

My dad and I both turn around to look at Marya. Her eyes are glowing like a heated pot of melted gold. Sweat has formed above her brows and she looks a little out of breath. Alec has an arm around her, working to help her get her strength back.

"I could feel her powers keeping me on the ledge," Tony tells us. He turns to Marya again. "Your gift is very powerful."

She blushes. "It was nothing."

Suddenly, the climb down makes more sense. I had no idea how Tony managed to keep us from falling that whole way down.

My dad wastes no time enveloping Marya in a rib-crushing hug. "It was everything. Thank you, Marya."

She looks up at my dad. I can see in her eyes that

the pride coming from a father figure means the world to her. I realize I know very little about Marya—like how long she's been without parents.

I walk over to her and give her a hug. "Thank you, Marya."

"You're welcome," she tells me and we smile at each other.

My dad turns back to Tony and pats him hard on the shoulder. It's like my dad is saying, *Welcome to the man club.*

Carrie brings Sabby over to us. His eyes are red and swollen from crying. He holds his hands out for me to take him in my arms. "I so scared, Wello. So scared!" He sniffles.

I pull him tighter to me. "I know, buddy. I was too. I'm okay though," I tell him.

"I know. Tony an Marra are heroes!" he says, mispronouncing Marya's name.

"Yes, they are." I smile at Tony from over Sabby's shoulder.

Growing weak, I hand my brother to my dad. Feeling the adrenaline crash, I allow myself to fall down to the ground and sit with my arms wrapped around my legs. I'm shaking from head to toe and I can't seem to stop. Everyone takes their turns coming over to Tony and me. I get a lot of hugs. Tony exchanges some manly handshakes and pats on the back. Everyone gives Marya her due attention too.

Eventually we all end up sitting on the ground, most of the others talking enthusiastically about how brave

Tony was and how powerful Marya's gift is.

I close my eyes and lean my head back, trying to get the shaking to stop.

I utilize my healing ability and Tony chimes in and helps. Eventually, my body begins to calm as it realizes that the imminent danger is gone.

"Feeling better?" Tony asks me quietly.

I wipe my hands on my jeans and nod my head. "Yes, I think it all caught up with me." I give him a half smile.

He puts his arms around me and pulls me closer to him. "I'm sorry about the rope. I had no idea that it would break like that. If I'd known, I would have never have let you or anyone else on it."

"It's not your fault that Alec exceeded the maximum weight limit, Tony," Connor—who shouldn't be honing in on our conversation—teases. Lillie is at his side, hanging onto his leg. She giggles at her brother's comment.

Alec punches him in the arm. "Whatever, Fatty Patty. You were the last one on that rope!"

Lillie laughs harder and Alec smiles down at her. He holds his hand out for her to give him a high five. She slaps her little hand against his and they exchange a fist bump. The humor in her expression drops and she looks up at her brother. Her little, black eyes look worried.

I instinctively turn my attention to Connor, whose face has gone white. Not because he feels bad, but because he's just realizing it could have been him falling from the cliff.

Tony—who shouldn't be listening in on Connor's thoughts—weighs in. "Yeah, I like you and all, Connor, but it would have been mighty awkward to have had to carry *you* down on my back." With that, the tension is cut.

Connor laughs and shakes off his feelings. I notice that Lillie's eyes lighten up as well. I wonder how hard it must be for her to have the empathic gift. It was hard enough for me to control how I dealt with feeling other people's emotions in the beginning. I can't imagine having to deal with it at such a young age like she does.

"Kids are resilient," Tony says inside my head.

I look from Lillie to Sabby and nod my head. "They sure are," I whisper. "Let's build a bridge," I say loud enough for everyone to hear.

"Heck yeah, I haven't tried this gift out yet," Tony adds, rubbing his hands together.

I think of how, with my gifts, I rarely knew how to work them in the beginning. In fact, most of the time I didn't even realize I could do something until it happened. Tony doesn't seem to have that much of an issue with anything like I do. A small spark of envy comes to me but I quickly extinguish it.

"What can I say? I'm a prodigy," Tony says in my head.

I raise an eyebrow at him. *"We'll see about that,"* I reply, remembering how telekinesis was one of the hardest gifts for me to master. I felt so out of control when I was using it and at first, it only came out naturally when I was in a situation with heightened emotions.

We hike over to where several gigantic tree trunks

lay in a pile under a few inches of snow. They measure to what I would estimate to be sixty feet in length. With the branches cleared and perfect cuts, I can tell that a machine took these down a while ago. My only question would be how they got machinery down here, but I guess that's better thought out for another day.

Tony stares down at the trees with a focused expression. We all watch him in silence as his body goes rigid with concentration. I keep looking back and forth from Tony to the tree and then back at Tony. He clenches his hands and perspiration begins building on his forehead, despite the arctic temperatures. The wood doesn't move an inch.

I put my hand on his shoulder a moment later and he relaxes his body. He turns to look at me. There is a gold swirl running through his irises but not nearly enough to give him the strength to move such a large object with his mind. "This one took me a while too," I tell him with a soft smile.

"Well, I guess even I have to have an Achilles heel." He smiles.

Much to my relief, he doesn't seem embarrassed or defeated. "It'll just take some practice. Perhaps start with a pencil or something that isn't ten times your body weight," I tease.

He grunts and then turns his attention back to the pile of wood. I turn as well to find that one of the tree trunks at the top has started shaking. We all back up and watch Marya. With seemingly no effort, she starts moving one of the trunks away from the pile. We watch her in awed silence while she slowly positions it to where it lays perfectly over the river. The process takes about ten minutes in all as she finagles it just right so that it doesn't end up crashing to the bottom of the riverbed.

"That's so cool!" Connor says with his eyes wide. Then his face goes pouty. "I wish I could do something as cool as that." He kicks the dirt in frustration.

"Walking through objects is just as cool, babe." Claire pats her man on his shoulder consolingly.

He perks up and shrugs his shoulders. "You're right. I am pretty awesome." He cocks a half-smile at Claire.

I laugh and roll my eyes. What a goober. "My turn," I say as I step up to the pile of wood. I focus on channeling my telekinesis gift as I stare at one of the logs at the top of the pile. A gold haze starts to rim the outermost parts of my vision. I focus harder and watch the log vibrate. It takes several minutes for me to get it off the pile of wood. My breathing is labored and sweat is accumulating on my brow. This sucker is heavy. Or, I've just been using my gifts too much these past few days and I'm a bit weakened by the over-usage.

Tony puts his hand on my shoulder and I suddenly feel a burst of strength. The large tree trunk floats in the air and I maneuver it to lay next to the other one across the riverbank.

I let out an exerted breath and wipe my forehead. "Thanks, babe," I tell Tony. He smiles.

"My tun!" Sebastian calls out.

Ending ELE

We turn to look down at the little guy who is standing tall with his hands on his hips in a Superman sort of pose. You can't help but smile and giggle a bit at how serious his little face is.

"It's awfully heavy, son," our dad tells him.

Sabby's eyebrows crease inward as he turns to look at our dad. "I so stwong!" he says and flexes his arm muscles to show us. Even though he has a jacket on and it would be impossible to see the bulge, I know it's there. I just don't know if my little brother could lift something that could be well over several thousand pounds.

My dad's look turns from humor to concern. "I don't want you to hurt yourself though, buddy."

"I no hurt myself. I stwong." He does his Superman pose again.

Then without waiting for my father's approval, he darts towards the logs, using his gift of speed. We watch in dumbfounded silence as he picks one of the logs off from the side of the pile. He gets behind one end and starts lifting it up, moving further towards the middle as he gets the trunk off the ground little by little. My eyes are open so wide that I can't even blink. He manages to push it to the bank of the river. Then he works the trunk up to where it is standing straight up in the air.

For a second I get a sickening fear that the tree trunk—that is several times taller than my little brother is—will fall on him. It doesn't though. Instead, Sebastian balances it just right so it stands without his effort. He steps slightly away from the trunk and, with a push of his index finger, he sends it falling. He darts to my side while the tree is still in mid-fall. A second later, it crashes down across the river. A huge spray of water flies in the air and the ground shakes from the impact.

I realize my mouth has been open during the entire process. Wide-eyed, I look around at my friends, at Tony, and at my dad. All of us wear the same expression of pure amazement.

Sabby giggles. "Toll you," he says in a cheerful tone, wagging his finger at me. He stands proudly once more, looking at all of us until my dad scoops him up in a giant bear hug.

My dad shakes his head in awe. "Wow, son! You weren't kidding…you *are* stronger than Superman!" My dad beams with pride.

"I know," Sabby says smiling, hooking his thumbs in his belt loop and rocking back on his heels.

"Way to go, Sabby!" Lillie holds her right hand up in the air for Sabby.

My little brother gives her a high five and then… winks at her? That sends an eruption of giggles from the crowd.

Tony ruffles the top of Sebastian's curls. "You are quite a champ."

"Yes! I can do anyfing." He smiles very big and stands even taller.

Tony raises his eyebrows at him with a humorous smile. "I bet you can. Do you want to help me secure the bridge?" he asks him.

My little brother's big, neon-yellow eyes light up and he nods his head with eager enthusiasm.

"Give me just a second." Tony quickly crosses the bridge to the other side, checking for its sturdiness. He returns a moment later seemingly confident that it's safe for my little brother.

"Alright, follow me," Tony says. He gestures with his hand for Sabby to follow as he trots over to the newly made bridge, making sure it's safe for all of us to cross. Sabby stays close behind Tony, mimicking his every move. Every once in a while, Tony looks back to make sure that Sebastian is safe and still following him closely. I see an amused expression on his face when he turns around one final time to look down at him. Then Tony climbs to the middle of the bridge and, seeing that Sebastian's close behind, he stops, runs in place, does ten jumping jacks, and sprints to the end of the logs, jumping off for a final effect.

I look at him in confusion, trying to figure out what the heck he's doing.

"*Watch*," I hear him say in my head. Without asking, I know he means to watch Sebastian. I turn my attention to my little brother. Then it dawns on me; Sebastian is going to copy what Tony just did—or is he? He is still standing in the middle of the logs with a look of utter confusion on his face. I see him take a deep breath, shrug his shoulders, and then he's off to the races. He runs as fast as his little legs can go, does ten jumping jacks…well, as good as a youngster can manage, then sprints off the log and jumps into Tony's waiting arms.

A smile spreads across my face. *Someday that may be our own child he's catching.* I shake my head, embarrassed for even having that thought. Tony looks up and meets my eyes from across the river in that same moment. I feel the warmth flooding to my cheeks, knowing he heard me. Tony just smiles at me adoringly and winks at me in agreement.

My dad, who's been standing next to me, leans over and whispers in my ear. "Yep, he's a keeper." He playfully jabs me with his elbow in my side and I can't help but laugh.

"Dad!" I say, feigning embarrassment.

All the rest of us make our way over the bridge. At the end, Tony takes my hand and helps me step down off the logs.

"The cabin should be only a little ways to the west of here," Tony tells me.

I nod my head and look up at the sky. The snow is starting to fall again. I hope it won't get as bad as it did yesterday.

"Wello! Wello!" I hear a little voice call from my side. I turn and find Sebastian with his hands in the air. I grab him in my arms and we continue walking towards the cabin. All the while, I'm praying we're going the right way.

We wade through the snow like a duck wading through water. The snow is still pretty deep and continuing to accumulate. I'm hoping that maybe the weather will warm up a bit in the next few days so the snow can begin to melt. I feel chilled to the bone and I almost find myself wishing for the crazy high temperatures that we had when they first implemented Project ELE.

After an hour or so of hiking, Tony reaches for Sebastian and places him on his shoulders. Sabby giggles at being so high up. He reaches his hands towards the sky and slaps the tree branches in the air as we go by. One of the branches must have been packed with snow, because Sebastian hits it and a huge wad of snow lands on Tony's head. I can't hold back the laugh as Tony becomes a human snowman. Tony tickles him and Sabby wiggles in delight.

Tony passes me a sideways glance and smiles. Grabbing my hand in his, he starts walking again. I look back at the others who are with us and notice my dad and Carrie carrying on what looks to be a very interesting conversation. Carrie lets out a huge laugh and my dad smiles, a genuine smile…one that I haven't seen in a very long time.

Tony sets my brother down. Sabby runs over to tag Lillie and they run around us as we walk, playing their own game of tag. They can't run very far because of the snow being so deep. Lillie and Sabby alternate being 'it' every few seconds or so.

I look at everyone around me. Even in the snow, they all seem to be in pretty good spirits. Then I bite my lip because I know from experience that things just can't be going this well for this long. Something is bound to happen soon and it's going to discombobulate us all. Call me a pessimist, or a glass half-full kind of girl…but I'm just keeping it real.

Tony squeezes my hand, bringing me back to the present. Instinctively, he can tell that something is up. Thankfully, he doesn't ask questions or search my mind for answers.

After a few more minutes of walking, Tony stops. "The cabin should be around here somewhere." He looks around the landscape for a moment, lost in thought, trying to put the pieces together with what he saw from the binoculars back in the cave.

I try to look around but I didn't even see what he pointed out in the binoculars, let alone any sign of a dwelling place in this area.

We walk a few more steps before Tony shakes his head, looking perplexed. "No, I think we passed it."

"I didn't see any signs of a cabin," Alec says, scratching his head.

"It's very well hidden, at least from what I remember. We need to look closer," Tony answers while he turns around and starts doubling back.

We walk slowly, examining the landscape around us carefully. After we walk a few hundred yards, I make out something from the corner of my eye. I look a little closer and find something sticking out of the snow. It's small, red, and out of place. I wade through the snow so I can examine the little piece of red metal. My knee hits something in the ground just below the red flag-looking thing. I reach my hand out and gingerly touch the piece of metal. It takes only a second for me to grasp what this is. I start brushing snow off around the metal and find that it's screwed into the side of a brick base. I push more snow off the structure to find the black mailbox door.

"A mailbox," Tony says simply.

I turn and smile at him, then I look back at my dad. The memory of the few times I was allowed out of the house in the years prior to Project ELE, comes flooding back to me. I would walk with my dad each evening out to the mailbox. Together, we would take the mail from the box and place it in a sterilized bag. He would sometimes leave a letter or a small package in the mailbox for the postman. My dad would then allow me to raise the small, red flag that tells the postman that there's outgoing mail to be picked up. I always felt so official raising the little warning flag. It's strange thinking back on it now. I used to breathe in deeply on those short trips outside. I'd try to take in all the landscape I couldn't see from my windows. I used to wonder what life on the outside would be like if we didn't have to stay indoors all the time…Now I know. Sometimes I find myself longing for those times of simplicity—when even if everything *wasn't* all right in the world, in my child's mind, it was.

Tony puts his hand on my shoulder and gives it a squeeze. "The house must be down that way just a little," he states.

I begin to notice that the trees are spaced out in a way that tells us they line a trail, or a driveway. With the snow covering everything, those telltale signs are hard to spot. Walking around the mailbox, we gesture for the others to follow us. We walk a few yards before we see the outline of a fireplace breaking out from behind brush and overgrown trees.

"This is the place. This is it!" Tony says excitedly. He starts walking quickly towards it—a man on a mission. The closer we get, the more we can spot the features of the huge log cabin behind the vegetation and under the snow. It's just not noticeable from the road but up close, it's very much a house. Great camouflage—perfect for our situation.

There isn't an entryway on this side of the house. We walk around it to the back and find the porch. It wraps around the side of the cabin and is covered in snow. This side is much clearer and easier to see. Windows cover nearly every inch of the home along the porch. I turn to see the view that the owners must have built the house to capitalize on. Mountains for as far as you can see line the landscape, looking perfectly majestic in all their glory.

"It's unlocked!" Claire calls.

I turn to find Connor and Claire hustling inside with Lillie. "Wait, shouldn't we check it out first?" I yell.

"Nothing's here," Tony tells me. "I don't know how I know that, but I can feel that this place is empty and has been so for a while." He holds out his hand for me to take.

I nod my head and take his hand. If it's good enough for Tony, then it's good enough for me. Together, we follow the others inside.

The cabin appears to be much larger than it looked on the outside. The windows give it plenty of natural light. Ceilings that soar up to a large skylight give it a grandiose appeal. Alec and Marya start pulling the white dust covers off all of the furniture. The rich, leather furniture and high-end accessories tell me that this home belonged to some people that were quite well off.

"I wonder who lived here," Mayra says in wonder after she pulls a dust cloth off a large china cabinet filled with silver and fine china.

"I don't know but I hope their propane tank is still in working order," my dad calls from the other side of the room. He's standing next to a gorgeous, double-sided fireplace that divides the living room and formal-dining room. River rock covers the outside of the fireplace and reaches all the way to the ceiling, giving a warm accent to the room. My dad flips a switch next to the fireplace. Nothing happens. He grabs a long lighter from the mantel, lights it, and places it over the gas logs. A second later, the gas catches flame and the fireplace lights up the room with an orange glow.

"Sweet!" Connor says. He takes Claire and they sit in a large, oversized chair next to the fireplace. Connor rubs his hands to get warm and Claire snuggles close to him.

I smile when I see Lillie walk up to them. Her freckled face looks a little unsure, but when Connor pats his leg, her face lights up and she climbs into the chair with them. They sit together like a small family. Claire says something that makes Lillie giggle. Lillie shows Claire how one of her front teeth is loose. Claire and Connor both appropriately ooh and ah and congratulate her on her upcoming loss of her first tooth, promising her a trip from the tooth fairy.

"This kitchen is drool worthy!" Carrie calls out from another room. "And it has a gas stove!" she exclaims.

I walk past the formal-dining room that has an exquisite chandelier hung low over a long, mahogany table that sits at least twenty. Several dust cloths cover large paintings in the room. The kitchen is just beyond it. I walk into the room to see Carrie gushing over the industrial-sized, stainless steel appliances, the tall, cherry-wood cabinetry, and the black, granite counters. The kitchen island has a pot rack hanging over it, filled with expensive copper pans and pots. Colorful, yet tasteful dishes are displayed in some of the glass front cabinets, giving a splash of liveliness to the room. A small kitchen table sits in a nook that has bay windows facing the mountains. "It's beautiful!" I tell Carrie.

She smiles with excitement. "I've only seen kitchens like this in magazines or on those fancy cooking shows. I've always wanted to have one."

"Well, now you have one," my dad says to her.

"This place is hardly mine," she says with a playful pout.

"I don't see anyone claiming it," my dad tells her.

She grins. "I could sleep in here."

"That wul hurt your booty, Ms. W," Sabby says to her.

She gushes at him, then continues perusing the cabinets and drawers, oohing and ahhing over the fancy gadgets and appliances.

"Check this out!" Alec calls from the other side of

Ending ELE

the house.

Tony and I walk together back through the living room and near the front door. A staircase leads to the top level of the home and another long hallway leads to a door just behind the staircase. Alec is inside the room behind the stairs. I walk in to find a fancy office and library. It smells like leather and cigars from a long history of smoking indoors. You can tell the room definitely belonged to a man. Dark browns, blacks, and greens make up the furnishings. A spiral staircase leads to an upper level of the library. A tall ladder connected to a track in the ceiling allows someone to access the books that are up high.

Connor runs into the room and jumps on the ladder. He goes sliding across the length of the bookcase.

"You're such a dork," Alec jabs.

"Proud of it," Connor says as he leans away from the ladder like Belle from Beauty and the Beast.

Claire climbs up the spiral staircase and examines the books up top. "Boring. These are all medical and science books." She climbs back down.

All of us busy ourselves snooping around at the gadgets and odds and ends on the shelves and on top of the desk. Connor picks up a pipe, puts it in his mouth, and pretends like he's studiously smoking it.

"Elementary, my dear Watson," Connor says with a mock puff.

We all turn to look at him in confusion. What a totally random statement, even for Connor.

"What?" He pulls the pipe out of his mouth to

speak. "My dad collected classic novels. You've never heard of Sherlock Holmes?"

We all shake our heads in unison.

"Well never mind then." He happily raises the pipe back to his lips and we all return to our search.

Another, smaller fireplace is next to the desk. Marya walks over to it and starts pulling the dust cloth off a framed picture above the mantel. A second later, the cloth drops to the ground and she gasps.

I look over at her. She's trembling and staring with wide eyes at the painting. I look up at it and something lurches in my stomach. My heart begins beating double time as I stare at the portrait in horror.

Connor lets the pipe drop from his lips and he spits several times, like it had some sort of disease on it.

Tony comes to my side and puts his arm around me to lend me his strength. "I had no idea this was his house."

I can't avert my eyes away from the oil painting of a family dressed in pristine clothes with serious expressions. The Hasting's family. Dr. Hastings stands shoulder to shoulder with his late wife, whom I never met in person. In front of them, sitting in chairs, are Candy and Zack. They are the only two people in the portrait to have a somewhat smile etched on their faces. Their eyes are their natural color and they look younger, like this was painted several years prior. I shiver, realizing that three of the four people in that painting are no longer living. "This is the Hastings's home." I say the obvious with a tremor in my voice.

"I'm so sorry. I didn't know." Tony pulls me closer

to him.

I shake my head in disbelief. "You couldn't have known. What are the odds though?" I ask.

"A million-trillion to one," Connor interjects.

The tension is thick in the room. Marya, having recovered from her shock, begins covering the picture up again. Claire jumps in and helps her.

My heart finally begins calming once the picture is no longer in view. I want to leave this room. I kind of want to leave this house but we have taken up so much time finding it already and it's not like the owners are coming back. Plus, Tony had a vision of us here. It's technically safe and an ideal location for a hideaway. I try shaking off the creepy feelings.

Connor is the first to get back to snooping around. "That's why he has all these science books." Connor looks at the books on the wall again. Then he turns around and leans back against the bookcase. "Ahh!" he yelps as the shelf he's leaning against begins moving backwards.

Claire grabs his arm just in time to keep him from falling down when the bookshelf mysteriously opens up a panel in the wall.

We all inch closer together around the secret chamber Connor discovered. Alec goes back to the desk and rummages through the drawers. He comes back with a flashlight and shines it inside the dark abyss.

The stairs lead downward toward some sort of secret basement. "This must be the basement from your vision," I tell Tony.

He shakes his head. "No, that one had a normal door and was off the kitchen. I didn't see this place."

"Well, let's check it out," Alec suggests.

Claire goes and closes the door to the office first. "I just want to make sure the kids don't come running in here and accidentally fall down the stairs."

"Good thinking," Marya tells her.

I smile at her maternal instincts.

"Boys first." I gesture to Alec.

He cautiously starts leading the way down the stairs. At the bottom, we find yet another door. Alec tries opening it. "It's locked," he says.

"I got this," Connor says. He steps through the door, using his powers. I hear a rustling and a few grunts on the other side as I assume Connor is trying to find the lock in the dark. A second later, the door is opened from the inside.

"Good job, babe," Claire tells him.

He beams with pride.

Alec shines his flashlight in the room and looks around for a light switch. With all the natural light up on the main floor, I hadn't even thought to try a light switch. It's been so long that we've been without electricity. I assume though, that at some point, Dr. Hastings would have made sure that there was power running to his home again. My stomach clenches as I think of him and whether he stayed here while he was holding our people hostage.

Marya spots the light switch first and flips it on. The room floods with a bluish white light, illuminating the lab. All kinds of electrical equipment, medical charts, and devices fill the room. An operation table sits on one side. A desk and workspace with two computers is on the other side. Beakers and testing equipment sit on an island workspace in the middle of the room.

"Creepy," Connor says.

"Yep," Tony agrees.

The question remains in the air as to why Dr. Hastings would need an operating table in the basement of his house. I shiver. I don't need to wonder why Dr. Hastings felt the need to have a secret lab. Nothing he did seemed to be much on the up and up.

We all branch off from each other and take turns scouring the room. I immediately head to his desk and search for any information that could be useful to us. I can't help but notice that his desk is meticulously clean. Everything has a place and is organized just so. I open the drawers and find a bunch of files. Nothing seems interesting to me at first, just files on family matters and finances. I can feel Tony behind me before I can see him.

"That drawer is too shallow," he states. I step off to the side as Tony steps in, examining the drawer. He begins pulling out the drawers at the top and setting them off to the side. He shimmies under the desk like an auto mechanic would a car and runs his hands along the surfaces. After a few minutes, he has an audience. All of us gather around Tony to see what he uncovers. I hear some sort of click. He gets out from under the desk and places one of the drawers back in place. Then he pulls it out halfway. Another click is heard and then Tony opens the original drawer the rest of the way, revealing another round of files.

"Seriously Tony, that's like the coolest thing you ever did. Very James Bond." Connor pats Tony on the shoulder.

"Yeah, that was pretty boss," Alec adds.

Tony grins and I can't help but smile at him. I know he hasn't officially been deemed "one of the guys," yet. Moments like this tell me that it might not be too long before Alec and Connor's bro-pack grows a little larger.

I inch closer to examine the contents of the drawer. A stapler, box of pens, and seven manila colored files are all that sits in it. Ignoring the office supplies, I pull the files out and place them on the desk. I bet Dr. Hastings is rolling over in his grave right now! We each grab a few of the files and surf through the contents.

"It's just a bunch of formulas, tax documents, and such," I announce rather bitterly. Just when I thought we had something. The only interesting thing I see is what looks like a code to some type of safe or something that is written by hand at the bottom of an instruction manual for the operating table. It's a series of four, two-digit numbers. We haven't seen any type of safe around here yet, so it's pretty much useless thus far.

We all throw the files back together, leaving them on the desk this time. Connor announces what's on everyone's mind. "I'm starving."

Feeling a bit defeated, we head upstairs, close the secret bookshelf, and wander towards the kitchen. It doesn't take long for the smell of pancakes to drift towards our noses. Instinctively, we rush quicker towards its origin.

Ending ELE

Inside the kitchen, we find Carrie flipping a golden pancake in the air like a pro. It lands back down on the skillet with a sizzling sound. Without taking her eyes from the stove, she answers our unasked question. "I found some wheat flour and other staples in the pantry. I was pretty sure you guys would be hungry so I whipped up some pancakes. I hope you all don't mind."

"Mind?" Connor says in mock shock. "As long as it isn't sauerkraut, I'm game!" I try to stifle a grin but fail. Connor puts his two fingers to his eyes again and moves them in Tony's direction. "I haven't forgotten," he says. To make it even funnier, he further clarifies his gesture. "Meaning, I'm watching you and when the time comes, you're getting yours." He clamps a fisted hand into his open hand.

Tony's eyebrows raise a quarter of an inch to let him know, 'Game on.'

I love these guys. Humor is a great distraction from the hectic world we live in.

Claire, Marya, and I help find some plates and forks for everyone. My dad comes into the kitchen with Lillie and Sabby in tow. Their little cheeks are rosy red from being outside.

"We foun a twampoline!" Sabby declares excitedly.

Lillie nods her head with equal enthusiasm. "It was awesome, Coco!" Her little, red curls bounce against her head as she runs to her brother's side.

"That sounds like fun! You'll have to take me there later," Connor tells her with a hug.

"Deal!" She smiles.

We take a seat around the kitchen table. My dad insists that Carrie take a seat and let him serve us. "You did all the cooking, so you get first dibs!" he tells her.

She smiles. "I like these rules!"

Alec comes to the table holding a jar over his head like a trophy. "I found some maple syrup! I don't know how old it is, but I don't think maple syrup goes bad." He sets the jar on the table.

Carrie picks it up. "Oh, this is the real stuff. I never could justify paying fifteen dollars for such a small bottle. This is going to be good." She opens the jar and pours a liberal amount on her hotcakes.

After everyone's been served, we dig in, leaving our manners at the door.

Sebastian is less than thrilled with our table etiquette. "Slow down, Wello. You gonna choke!"

I purse my lips and smile. My mom was a horrible cook but she always made sure to teach us the proper way to eat a meal. I slow down and remember to actually chew my food—not inhale it.

Sabby nods his head as if to tell me, 'good job'.

Could he be any cuter? I watch him gingerly cut his pancakes with the side of his fork and stuff a small bite in his mouth. I wonder if he realizes that his birthday is only a day away. He hasn't mentioned it. Then again, we rarely ask what day it is. I haven't the slightest clue as to what we're going to do to celebrate. My mom used to make him birthday pancakes with icing and sprinkles. I wonder if that would be too much for him though…now that Mom's gone.

After we're done eating, we shoo Carrie out of the kitchen and take on dish duty. It amazes me that running water is also available here. I guess Dr. Hastings still has the hook up…even after death. I push that thought out of my mind immediately—it sounds so morbid.

We spend the rest of the afternoon sifting through the house. We come up empty with anything that may leave us clues as to what happened with Project ELE or clues as to what our next move should be. It seems like we're running in circles; none of us are sure about what to do next. As the sun begins to set, we go in search of candles. It's one thing to have access to electricity, but another to use it in the dead of night. We don't want to light up the house like a Christmas tree and give the 'other guys' the location of where we are. We may as well send up fireworks if we did that.

After we put Sebastian and Lillie to bed, the rest of us congregate in the living room. Carrie made us all some hot tea, which is immensely soothing. I sit on Tony's lap on the floor of the living room. We've all brought down blankets to cuddle up with. While we've lit the fire and turned the heat up a bit, there is still a crisp chill to the air.

My dad's the first one to speak up. "We've had a pretty grueling last couple of days—er, well, a long year I guess." He clears his throat and continues. "But, as of now, I feel like we reflect some resemblance of safety being here. Now, having said that, I don't want us to put our guards down. I do, however, want to celebrate my little boy's birthday. He's had a rough year and even if it's just for a day, I want him to be a little boy and worry for nothing. In order to do this though, I'm going to need to enlist all of your help." He looks around the room at all of our smiling faces and nodding heads. There isn't anything I would love more than to make Sebastian's fifth birthday one he'll never forget. Even in these turbulent times, it's important to make memories.

We find a pad of paper and some pens and begin jotting down some ideas for what to do for Sabby's birthday. We don't have a whole lot to work with, being as though we're out in the middle of nowhere and only brought the necessities with us. However, we can use our imagination—which is something a five-year-old can certainly appreciate. After about a half hour or so, we've managed to compile a very long list of ideas, which are mostly games. It takes us another twenty minutes or so to narrow it down to our top five. Connor takes up most of our time trying to persuade us to keep no-rules dodge ball on the list. With as powerful as Sebastian is, that one seemed like a no-brainer to me that the game might end in complete disaster.

"Okay, so let me read off the final list," I tell everyone as we all quiet down. Connor folds his arms and huffs in the corner. He would have been creamed if we'd kept no-rules dodge ball so I'm not sure why he's huffing and puffing. Claire rubs his back as I continue. "We have: snow war, capture the flag, tag, red rover, red rover—which I'm still a bit wary of—and kick the can." I look up from my list and find everyone satisfied.

Alec interjects, "If we are going to have the snow war after Sebastian wakes up then we have a lot of work to do between now and then." I nod my head.

Carrie speaks up, "I can stay here with the little ones while the rest of you start making the forts. I can also take care of the meals."

"Thank you, Carrie!" I say. "That helps a lot." We all get up and stretch, then go to put on our snow gear.

Tony surprises me by coming up behind me and putting his arms around me. "Hey babe," he says, giving my neck a small but intimate kiss.

I squirm at his touch and giggle. "Hey yourself. You need to get ready; we have a lot of work ahead of us tonight."

He gives me another kiss or two and then lets me go to get his winter gear on.

It's a cold but pleasant evening. The wind is calm and the sky is clear. We bring out flashlights but don't have to use them—we work with the light of the moon. Carrie brings us out every Tupperware container she could find for us to use as brick molds. Our goal is to turn this yard area into a place any five-year-old would kill to be in. Snow forts of every shape and size every ten feet or so are planned to litter the yard. We work late into the night and start to finish at about five in the morning. We make a few hundred snowballs and place them in mounds at the larger snow forts. When we all step back to look at our work, we can't believe our eyes.

"This. Is. Totally. Awesome!" Connor exclaims, fist bumping the air. All the boys join in, hooting and hollering about their accomplishments.

The girls stand back and let them do their thing. "Men," Claire huffs jokingly. She makes me giggle.

We take our shoes off when we get in. Carrie is there to meet us with some hot tea and cocoa. While we warm our hands by the fire, we decide to take a quick nap before the little ones get up. Carrie is smart and says she put a heavy, black blanket over the window in their room to make them sleep longer. Genius. I fall asleep next to my best friend while counting all of my many blessings.

SIX

I wake up with a start as I hear my name.

"*Wello! Wello, wake up!*" I'm groggy and try to fall back asleep.

"Just a few more minutes," I mumble, half-asleep.

"Wello," the little, insistent voice bellows again. "It's my birday! I'm five years old, Wello, look!"

I peek out of one of my eyes and see Sabby's hand proudly displaying five fingers. "I'm a whole hand old, Wello!"

Claire giggles under her breath. I lick my lips and try to will my eyes to open.

"Time to get up," Carrie says. "I bought you till nine."

I groan and rub my eyes. Everyone shuffles around me, trying to come to. We only had a few hours of sleep but I guess it's better than nothing. I sit up and yawn big, stretching my arms to the ceiling. I would kill for a few more hours.

Sabby grabs my hand and pulls me to standing so fast I almost lose my balance. "Geeze boy, I forget how strong you are…"

Sabby flashes me a big smile as he pulls everyone else to a standing position, sleeping or not. He grabs Connor's hand while he is still sleeping and manages to get him to a standing position before he falls flat on his face. I nearly pee my pants from laughing so hard. Connor fails to find the humor in it all.

Sabby pulls me by the hand to the large window that overlooks the yard. "Lookie, Willow! It's so much fun!"

I lean down and pick up Sebastian. "Sabby, did you just say Willow?"

He grins. "Yep, cause today I'm a big boy."

I get a little teary-eyed. "Can you do me a favor, Sabby?" He nods his head. "Can you still call me Wello? Even though you're big, I like that name. It's kind of special to me."

He contemplates this for a moment and then nods. "K, W-E-L-L-O," he says, long and drawn out. He bursts out laughing like it's the funniest thing in the world. I set him down on the ground and he's off running again. I can't remember the last time I've seen him so happy and boisterous.

Carrie calls us in from the other room. "Time to eat!"

I bite my lip, worried that Sabby is going to miss his yearly breakfast from our mom. When I get into the kitchen though, he's already parked on top of a stool, devouring pancakes with little sprinkles.

I'm suddenly completely at awe. How on earth did Carrie pull this off? I turn and find her doing dishes at the sink. "Hey Carrie, where on earth did you get sprinkles?" I'm literally blown away.

She smiles at me. "I made them." She says this like it's the most natural thing in the world. She turns the water off and dries her hands. "Your dad told me yesterday about his traditional birthday pancakes with sprinkles. So, I just put some sugar and water together with a bit of food coloring I found in the pantry and voilà."

I shake my head and then wrap her in my arms. She returns the hug. "Thank you," I whisper to her. "You don't know how much this means to our family." And I mean it.

Lillie is the first to get done eating and hops down from her stool. She's playing with a small doll, one she must have found somewhere in the house. She makes it hop and jump from the couch, to the coffee table, and so on until she gets to the large, picturesque windows. I watch her as I take a bite of my pancake, noticing just how sweet and carefree she is.

Connor pokes me in the ribs with his fork. "Now you know where she gets her good looks from," he says slyly.

I roll my eyes. "Yeah, sure," I tease. I look back at Lillie, who has since dropped the doll. The doll lies on the floor in an awkward position, as Lillie is plastered to the glass.

"Sabby, Sabby," she says excitedly. "Sabby, come here, lookie! You have to see this!" She takes turns dancing around the living room and then plastering her little face back to the window.

Sebastian hops off the stool and goes running over. It cracks me up how kids are either running or sleeping. There's no in between. Sebastian joins Lillie by the window. He looks back towards us, to the window, back to us, and then bellows out the most excited scream you've ever heard. Soon they are both screaming, dancing, and begging to go outside and play.

Sebastian comes over to where I'm sitting, grabs my hand, and guides me over to look. As if I hadn't seen it before, I play along and act surprised by the forts. They do look even cooler in the daylight. The sunlight has broken through some of the clouds and shines off them, giving them a shimmery, ethereal quality.

Before long, Sebastian has managed to get everyone out of their seats and looking out the windows. We all join in, jumping around and yelling in excitement. Even my dad is being silly for Sabby's sake.

Connor's voice can be heard over everyone else's. "Oh my gosh! Forts!"

Sabby makes a b-line for his stuff and starts getting his coat, gloves, and hat on. He manages to get his galoshes on the wrong feet, which makes me giggle. We all rush to our things to get our snow gear out. Sebastian stands at the window, jumping up and down while we finish getting geared up. He wastes no time opening the door and running outside. Carrie comes up behind Sebastian and begins tying a blue ribbon around his head.

"What you do that for, Ms. Carrie? I not a girl!"

Ending ELE

Carrie giggles. "No Sebastian, you're not. But how else are you going to be able to tell whose team you're on?"

Sabby's face scrunches up while he contemplates this. Then he smiles. "Ms. Carrie, you so smart!"

We break off into two almost-even teams, blue and red. Tying the ribbons to our head, we run to our appointed forts. Tony grabs Sebastian's hand and leads him to the middle of the fort area. He kneels down and talks with Sabby for a moment and we all wait. Then the two of them stand up. Sebastian is sporting a very cocky grin, which makes me worry what the two of them were discussing. Tony calls out the instructions for the game. "The game is: Capture the Flag. The goal is to—capture the flag. So, since it's Sebastian's birthday, I've decided to let him call the rules—so here they are. Rule number one, have fun. Rule number two, if you have any questions, refer back to rule number one." He looks around at all of us and I wait for him to say something else.

"Wait," I say aloud. "You're telling me that there are *no* rules? That it's an all-bets-are-off snowball fight?" I'm exasperated! With everyone's abilities, there's no telling what might happen.

Of course, Tony has read my thoughts and says aloud, "Correct. There are *no* rules." He cocks me a smile and leans down to tell Sebastian something in his ear. Whatever it was must have been funny because Sabby giggles and then looks at me. My face heats up as everyone stares at me. I've decided to accept the fact that I am officially screwed. He's got an invisible girl, a super boy, a girl who can move anything with her mind, and to top it off, Tony can do all of the above. *Great!*

"You have thirty seconds to get to your forts before we start. The time starts.... now!"

We waste no time getting into our groups. I have my dad, Connor, Lillie, and Alec on my team. We put our heads together for a very quick planning meeting.

"Needless to say, we're up the creek, unless you've got some brilliant idea, Willow," Connor says.

I think for a moment, realizing they're asking me to take the lead. I try to think it over really fast. We have one more than they do but we also don't have the most useful power wielders on our team. My dad can use his gift of vision to perhaps see their moves in advance. That is, if he can get it to work that way. Connor can walk through walls, which may prove to be useful. Alec can heal, but I'm not sure how that would really help us. He's smart though. Lillie can feel other's emotions. I have no idea how to make that work in our favor. "Okay, we need a steady supply of ammunition. Dad, can you handle snowball-making duty and watching the flag?"

He nods his head and shrugs his shoulders. "Yeah, sure. I can do that."

I smile and nod my head. "Good, Lillie, can you use your adorable cuteness to walk around and act like you're not doing anything? We need you to be our secret weapon. If you are able to walk close, but not too close, to their forts, to hear about any plans they've have, that would help huge."

Ending ELE

Lillie pulls the doll she was playing with earlier out of her pocket. "I've got this," she says while smiling sweetly. Something tells me that Lillie might be a lot more tenacious than her innocent appearance lets off. She skips out in to the open with her doll and looks every bit like a little girl who's not interested in this game.

"Connor and Alec, how do you feel about being the enforcers? Connor, you can stay near the fort and help my dad protect the flag. Alec, you can come along with me and we can try to steal their flag."

"On it!" Connor and Alec say at the same time while doing some kind of macho handshake.

A whistle blows and fake battle cries erupt in the air.

"Let's do this!" I call. My dad and Connor both drop to start forming snowballs. My dad already has a good-sized pile ready for us that he made while I was divvying out tasks. Alec and I grab as many as we can fit in our arms and start running. I turn us both invisible and Alec struggles to keep ahold of me to stay invisible, while holding onto the lot of snowballs.

We peek around the corner and I see Claire and Marya working their way stealthily across the battlefield. Claire is helping Marya stay invisible, but of course, I can see the two of them. I dart my eyes around, looking for Tony, knowing that only he can see through our invisibility. I don't catch sight of him.

The first snowball is launched towards our fort by Claire. It looks like it came out of nowhere but it's aimed directly for Connor. It hits the intended target smack dead in the face.

From where I stand, I can see the surprise in his expression. He knows exactly who's responsible for it too. "Thanks a lot, babe!" he calls out, waving his hand in the air, pieces of snowball dripping from his hair. I can read his intentions from the emotions coming from him. So I wait to see it unfold.

Claire remains invisible but giggles nonetheless. That's all Connor needs to make a good estimate of her coordinates. He pulls two snowballs out from behind his back and chucks them down at her. The first one misses and the other hits her in the shoulder.

She throws her hands on her hips, which brings Marya into full view. "I thought you loved me!" she pouts jokingly.

Taking advantage of the moment, Marya starts concentrating on the flag. I watch as it shakes back and forth a little and begins to levitate up from the fort.

"Dad!" I call out, giving away our position. A spraying of snowballs comes toward me from around the corner of the other team's fort. By the sting that they leave, I know they are coming from my little brother. I take cover behind a tree.

I look over at my fort just in time to see my dad grab ahold of the flag to keep it from flying away. I smile. Alec leaves my side and runs towards Marya, who is still trying hard to make the flag move, even if it means moving my father with it. She doesn't see Alec until it's too late. He tackles her playfully to the ground. They both laugh and try to shove snow at each other.

    Claire makes a run for our fort and I go for her fort. I still don't know where Tony is and I'm a little nervous about getting any closer to my little brother. If I thought that it hurt to be pinged by snowballs from a distance, imagine how much it would hurt up close. Too bad there isn't a Major League anymore because Sabby would be an all-star pitcher.

    I see my brother's curls from around the corner of the fort and I dodge in time to miss the curve ball he sends my way. A flash of red hair tells me that Lillie is coming up from behind him. All of a sudden, my brother erupts into a ferocious round of the giggles. He starts laughing so hard that he drops the snowballs in his hands and falls to the snow-cushioned ground. He starts rolling back and forth laughing.

    I can't help but laugh at the incredulousness of it. What in the world is *that* funny? I see Lillie standing behind him. An intense look of concentration is on her face. She obviously didn't say or do anything funny. Her eyes look blacker than ever as she stares down at my brother. It creeps me out a bit but I don't sense any maliciousness coming from her. *What on earth?* I wonder.

    I tune into my brother's emotions long enough to realize what's going on. She's forcing these feelings on him. I never thought of humor as an emotion, but it is one. She is filling him with humor and cheerfulness to the point that he can't stop laughing. I smile and shake my head in awe. This girl might just be a lot stronger than any of us could have imagined.

With my little brother taken care of, I run towards their fort. The chaos of the snowball fight ensuing behind me gets quieter as I near the edge of the opposing team's fortress. All is too calm for me to let my guard down. The biggest question of all is—where's Tony? I try to send out some feelers to listen for thoughts or feelings coming from him, but I get nothing.

I stop stealthily at the edge of the fort with my back against the snow-bricked wall. I listen but hear nothing. It's now or never. I brace and arm myself with two snowballs before turning the corner. The flag is only a few feet in front of me and nobody is around to protect it. I tiptoe as quietly as I can towards the pole, excited to be so close. I reach my hand out to grab the blue flag.

"You're cute when you're trying to be sneaky," Tony says. He's so close to me that I can feel his breath on my neck and it sends a delightful shiver through me.

I raise my hands in mock surrender and slowly turn around to face my not-so-much enemy. I look up into his eyes, which are swirled with a handful of colors that he's been using for the game.

He gives me a breathtaking smile that is hot enough to melt the fort to the ground. "So, you want my flag?"

I nod my head impishly.

"And you expect me to let you just—take it?" he asks in a mischievous whisper.

I nod my head again, biting my lip. My heart has picked up its pace and the heat has filled my cheeks. How is it that Tony can make me melt like this still? I wonder if the intense attraction I have for him will ever settle with time.

"That's very doubtful," he says, answering my private thoughts. He pulls me into a kiss that warms me from the inside out. I lose myself for that minute we are so close that nothing can pull us apart. Our hearts are beating at the exact same rhythm and I know then that they are connected in a way that could never be separated. I'm left breathless when he pulls away just enough to whisper in my ear again. "Please don't be mad."

I pull my head back, confused, and that's when I hear something rustling behind us. I turn around to see Marya tying our red flag just below their blue one. She is blushing from being an obvious witness to our intimate moment.

I turn and glare at Tony but my heart's not really into it. Instead, I laugh and push him to the ground, using my strength. Dropping down above him, I start shoveling snow all over him. I try to push some down his jacket and we end up wrestling on the ground playfully in an all-out snow fight. I can hear my team members booing and Tony's team members whooping and hollering. All of a sudden, the fort is being busted down as my team starts pulling it apart. I use my telekinesis gift to burst it apart and snow bricks go flying into the air. We all laugh and hit each other with snow in every which way. Nobody cares whose team they're on. It's every man for themselves as the front yard is filled with chaos.

After another twenty minutes of our anarchic snow war, we run inside chilled to the bone. Carrie is ready for us as we enter. Towels are laid out on the floor so we don't slip on the melting snow that drops from our outerwear. We dress down from our outside clothes, greedily sip hot cocoa, and slurp the hot ramen that she spoons out into our bowls.

Everyone's eyes are so alight with giddy excitement and happiness that it's so easy to forget all that is wrong in our worlds. For one day, everything is right. Everything is good as it should be. We are kids like we are meant to be. Even the adults look ten years younger.

We spend the remainder of the day playing our favorite childhood games and by the time it gets dark, everyone is exhausted but happy. For dinner, we have spaghetti, which is one of Sebastian's favorites. He smiles as he slurps up a noodle loudly.

"This is one of the best birthdays ever!" he says. Then his eyes grow sad for a second. "I wish Mom were here."

My dad pulls his chair closer to him and puts an arm around his shoulder. "She is. She's watching you from the best place in the world—Heaven."

Not hearing our change of conversation, Carrie comes to the table with a cake that holds five candles.

Sabby nods his head and looks to my dad. "Do you think if I use my wish to bring her back, it would work?"

My dad's mouth drops and his eyes turn sad. He looks to me and then to Carrie, not sure how to answer that. How do you tell a child that those kinds of wishes are impossible?

I try to help. "Are you tired, Sabby?"

He looks at me confused because my question makes no sense. "A little."

"Do you ever feel sad?" I ask.

"Sometimes," he answers, furrowing his eyebrows.

"What if you were in a place that you never got tired? Or you would never get sad? Instead, you would always feel happy; you would always feel healthy. What if every day it was the perfect temperature, the sun always shined on you, and you were able to bask in it to enjoy every ounce of life because you had no fear, you had no concerns, no worry, nothing to trouble you? What if anything you ever wanted was at your fingertips in this place?" I ask.

His eyes brighten. "Like this cake? I could always have cake?"

I nod my head. "Yes, you could in this place. Would you like that, Sabby?" I ask him.

He nods his head excitedly.

"Would you ever want to leave a place like that?" I ask him.

"No." He shakes his head, still slightly confused with where the conversation had gone.

"Well, Mom is in a place like that." My throat chokes with emotion. "You wouldn't want to ask her to leave such an amazing place, would you?" Tears fill my eyes, threatening to spill over.

His eyes water as well. A barrage of emotions

flickers over his face. He wants two things. He wants his mom for him and he wants his mom to be happy. "So I shouldn't wish for her to come back to us?" he asks me, unsure of himself.

I shake my head sadly. "No Sabby. We should let her be happy. Instead of wanting her to come down to us, we can look forward to the day that we go up to be with her, forever." I want to say so much more, but how do you explain everything to a five-year-old child?

"When would we go up to be with her?" he asks. A flicker of recognition suddenly crosses his face and he looks sad again.

"You have a long time before that. But if you are good, Sabby, you will see Mom again one day. When that day comes, you won't ever have to worry about losing her again," my dad answers for me.

"Okay," Sabby says as he stares at the dwindling candles on the cake. Two of them have extinguished. Carrie picks up a candle and uses it to relight the others.

"What should I wish for then?" Sabby asks.

"That's up to you," my dad tells him.

He nods his head and seriously debates this responsibility. I want badly to listen in to his thoughts and know what he's thinking, but I know that wouldn't be right. Sabby closes his eyes and a second later, he blows out the candles in one very strong breath. When he opens his eyes again, he has a huge smile.

"What did you wish for?" Lillie asks him.

"I not supposed to say," Sabby answers. His face is

back alight and no longer filled with a grief that a child should not have to endure.

We go with it and the room returns to its previous jovial atmosphere. After dinner, we clean up and head into the living room. When Sabby rounds the corner he squeals, "Presents!" He runs to the coffee table, where a few small, wrapped gifts are. He jumps up and down and Lillie joins in with his excitement.

"Go ahead and open them," my dad tells him.

Sabby doesn't wait. He grabs the first one from the pile.

"That one is from us," Alec and Marya share.

Sabby rips apart the makeshift wrapping, which is really a reused cereal box. He opens it up and finds a disk. He pulls it out and looks at it inquisitively. "What is it?" he asks.

Alec laughs. "It's a Frisbee. Have you never seen one before?" Sabby shakes his head so Alec continues in his explanation. "You throw it to someone and it kind of flies in the air. I'll show you how to use it tomorrow."

"Thanks!" Sabby runs to hug Alec and Marya. Then he runs back to the pile of presents.

He opens a present that has a book about dragons in it from Carrie next. "I found it in the attic," she tells him. He gives her a hug as well and flips through a couple of the pages, oohing over the pictures.

Connor and Claire give him an old action figure that has a sword and shield. They found it around the house and I try not to think that it may have belonged to a childhood Zack.

Lillie made Sabby a bracelet out of macaroni noodles and string. Sabby gave her a hug and I couldn't help but think how adorable they are.

My dad's present is a little larger. He found a skateboard in the attic and he promises to show Sabby how to use it. However, with the snow, they can only practice in the foyer or perhaps the kitchen. My dad knows that he probably won't be able to bring the gift with him if we go on the run again, but he figured that teaching him to ride would be more of the gift than the actual skateboard itself.

The last gift on the table is from Tony and me. We worked on it together last night. Sabby picks up a small envelope and begins opening it. He pulls out two small cards that could easily fit in his pocket. They are made of a thicker cardstock that we found in the office. He turns them over and smiles when he sees the first picture. He turns it around to show it to everyone. Tony drew a small portrait of my family, including my mom. Both my dad and I posed for him last night. He drew Sabby while he was sleeping. His memory of our mom was pretty accurate and his picture nearly brought her to life. It was so well drawn.

"Now you can keep us with you all the time," I tell Sabby.

He smiles and runs to give us both a hug. Remembering that there was another card, he turns it over to look at it. His eyes brighten and he smiles in excitement. "That me!" he declares.

Tony and I laugh, knowing what the picture looks like. The others ask to see it. Sabby turns the card around so we can all see Super-Sabby. Tony did a great job on the caricature that turned Sabby into Superman.

"Tank—Thank you!" he says excitedly to us.

"You are more than welcome. The drawings were your sister's ideas," Tony makes sure to tell him.

"Thank you, Wi…Wello!" He gives me a second hug.

"Anything for you, little bro," I tell him, ruffling his curls. I wonder if he will ever get sick of me doing that.

Sabby smiles big at all of his newly opened presents, then he reaches his hands over his head and yawns.

"Are you tired?" my dad asks him.

He shakes his head. "No. I five now. I don get tired."

We all smile adoringly at him. His little eyelids are heavy. Looking over at Lillie, we see she's already curled up on the couch, one little, freckled arm hanging off the side as she sleeps.

"How about I read you that book?" Carrie asks Sabby.

He picks the book up and clutches it to his chest as he nods, half-excitedly and half-sleepily. Carrie takes one of his hands and together they walk to the cot of bedding we made downstairs for him. We know there are more than enough rooms in this house, but our family still wants to be close to each other. After all, in times like these, you never know when you will have to rush out into the night. It's best not to have to go searching for everyone if that happens. The bottom story of the house is also much warmer than upstairs.

My dad rubs his shoulder and stands up. "I must be getting too old for this much excitement." He stretches and I can hear his joints pop.

I cross the room to give him a hug and with that hug, I send some of my healing power into him. He notices it, leans back, and says, "Perks of having a super daughter, huh?"

I shrug my shoulders and smile up at him. He ruffles my hair and much like old times, his fingers get caught amidst my unruly curls. We both laugh as he pries his fingers away. "Goodnight, Dad."

"Goodnight sweetie." He turns to everyone else, "Don't stay up too late."

"We won't," Claire assures him.

"Mmhm." He smiles at her and then to Marya before going to bed.

I can sense a feeling of belonging coming from both girls, who are fatherless. I also can sense that my dad knows now that his family is a whole lot bigger than it was before Project ELE.

After he leaves, the rest of us huddle around the fire for a few more minutes. I'm physically tired but my mind is still whirling at astronomical speeds. I can't stop thinking about Dr. Hastings's study.

"Do you want to go back and look around again?" Tony asks me.

The others look at us with interest since his question

Ending ELE

seemed to come out of nowhere. "Yeah, I don't think I'm going to be able to fall asleep right away anyhow," I answer.

"You do know that holding freaky, inner-mind conversations with each other is just as bad as whispering, don't you?" Connor says.

"Sorry. I was just listening to Willow's thoughts about Dr. Hastings and figured she might want to go back and look around again." Tony says.

"Do you always listen into each other's thoughts?" Marya looks inquisitively at us.

"I don't think I would like that," Alec adds. "Sometimes, the mind doesn't have the best things to say."

"We try not to," I say, looking over at Tony. "Sometimes it's hard to stay out though. It's kind of like a radio that's playing in the background. You don't even pay attention to it but every once in a while, a note will hit or an announcer will come on and say something that peaks your interest and you tune back in."

"Do your thoughts sound the same as your voice does?" Claire asks.

I hadn't really thought about that before.

Tony answers her. "It sounds a little different. It's hard to explain but it's like your thoughts are directly connected to your inner being. If you were to say something out loud, you would be careful how you phrase it, how much emotion you put into it, and how much volume you use. Inside your head, there is no filter. Your thoughts are raw, pure, and untainted. So naturally with that, you sound different than you do aloud." He turns to look me in the eyes. The intensity in his gaze has my stomach heating up. "To be able to hear Willow's innermost being is like being able to listen to the real ocean after you have only heard it through a seashell your whole life. It's capturing the most beautiful chords and strumming them in the most perfect of rhythms. It's ethereal."

To say that butterflies are running around my stomach would be an understatement. My stomach had long since fluttered away and is flying up, up, and into outer space. My cheeks are flushed and my heart is dancing about in my chest. I grab his hand gently, lacing my fingers with his. He leans towards me, presses his lips to mine, and for one second—we are flying.

"A-hum." Alec clears his throat.

...And with that, we are catapulted back to earth. Realizing that our PDA is directly in front of our friends, the blush sets in from head to toe. I lean back from Tony and push my hair behind my ears, keeping my eyes on the ground. Tony's hand is still laced in mine and I can feel his pulse thrumming wildly in his fingertips.

"That is so romantic," Claire says dreamily.

"I'll show you romantic," Connor says. He pulls Claire up to her feet, then dips her slightly over his arm and gives her a kiss like you would see in old movies. Her right foot even leaves the ground with that foot-popping kind of kiss.

I watch in amusement, half expecting that, in true Connor fashion, he would do something funny, like accidentally drop her or fall over or something.

Ending ELE

He doesn't falter but my dad does clear his throat from across the room, loudly enough for us to hear him. "Uh-uh!" he says, shaking his finger at Connor, who is looking at him with that deer-caught-in-the-headlights kind of expression. Poor Claire is still dipped in his arms.

"Yes sir." Connor rights Claire quickly and then like an admonished schoolchild, he puts a few inches of space between him and her and sits down.

I can't help but laugh and jab at him for getting caught.

"So, do you want to go snoop around some more?" Tony asks me.

"Heck yeah!" I say. We all get up to head over to Dr. Hastings's study. "We are going to go do some Nancy Drew-style investigating," I call to my dad as the guys walk in the direction of the study.

"Okay, but don't let those Hardy boys pull any more moves on my girls!" he says.

I laugh and so do Marya and Claire, who heard his comment. We three chime back at the same time, "We won't."

Connor pushes at the bookshelf, trying to get it to open again.

It doesn't budge.

"Maybe you pulled back on a specific book or something," Alec offers and starts pulling at books.

"He just leaned on it last time," I say.

"Well, something has to be the trigger," Alec says.

All six of us are looking around at the bookshelf, expecting to see a big, red, easy button. Marya is the one who ends up finding it, but it's not a button. Instead, it's a series of three large medical manuals that won't pull out from the shelf. When she pushes them in, the door opens. "That seems too easy," Marya says as we start walking down the dark stairwell.

"Yeah, it is, but who exactly would be looking for a secret panel? Secrets hidden in plain sight seem to be the best kept," I answer.

"True," she agrees.

The door at the bottom is still unlocked from yesterday. We go inside and flip on the light switch. We all start to scour the room again, looking for clues we might have missed.

Alec and Connor both try to get the computer to boot up, but soon find out that it's all password protected. After a few failed attempts of coming up with a passcode, they end up locking themselves out of the computer.

I head back over to the files on the desk and start leafing through them again. There isn't much useful information in it at all. *Sure, the documents have personal information on them, but why go through the trouble of hiding them in a secret drawer?* I wonder.

I pick up the instruction manual for the operating table again. I trace over the written code at the bottom with my thumb. The operating table has all types of electrical hookups and device inputs and outputs. I walk over to look at the operating table and end up staring at it for quite a while.

Tony comes up behind me and puts his arms around my waist. "Perhaps you're right."

I crane my neck to look up at him—our lips are only inches apart. It takes everything in me not to kiss him right then. "Do you think there's something to this table?"

"Let's find out." He walks towards the table. His eyes turn brown as he pushes his hand through the table, reaching right into the middle of it. I hadn't even thought of doing something so easy to find out if my hypothesis might be correct.

Less than a minute later, Tony pulls his hand out of the table and along with it, a silver, metal briefcase. He sets it on the nearby desk and I smile up at him in amazement. "Well, that was easy," I joke. "I might have stared at that table all night looking for some key to finding out if any secrets laid within it."

"But you didn't. We make a good team, you and me." He kisses me on the nose and gestures for me to open the briefcase. Sure enough, there is a number-coded lock that has exactly four sections for two-digit numbers. I enter the code that's on the manual and the briefcase clicks open.

"More papers, yippee!" I say unenthusiastically. I pull a stack out, hand a few to Tony, and we both sit on the floor, looking through everything.

This info is a little juicier. I find some correspondence between the FDA and Dr. Hastings. He sent in a detailed form requesting to be able to test out some sort of wonder drug on human subjects. The first correspondence dated back five years ago. It seems like they went back and forth with written correspondence asking for facts and figures of a long-term test on animals that Dr. Hastings didn't have at the time. As we later learned, he had only been testing his drugs on humans, including his wife and children. He didn't note those facts though. As the correspondence continued throughout the five years, his replies to the FDA's questions became more and more cynical. He answered them like he was obviously too brilliant to be wasting time on their dimwitted questions. The correspondence stopped about a year prior to Project ELE. "Well, it looks like the government never gave Dr. Hastings permission to test his so-called immunizations on the human populous," I say aloud.

"That doesn't surprise me," Tony says as he hands

me a new stack of papers. "Here is his application and acceptance letter for becoming the leader of the shelter here. Nothing states anything about injecting the populous with strange immunizations. In fact, it looks like he was given a detailed list of what immunizations would be given. They are the standard ones that anyone going into another country would be given. Also, if you read further, you will find that there is a bunch of stuff he didn't follow. Like the testing for example. That should not have taken as long as it did for people to gain entrance to the shelter. They estimated twenty-four to forty-eight hours at most for all citizens to finish testing. Also, the test to see if you have the virus seems to be a finger-prick blood sample. It's not nearly as in depth as the one that we were given. There were no shots that people who were infected were supposed to be given, like we were. They could be given antibiotics and a month's prescription of pain pills, but that was all. Then to top it all off, the protocol specifically stated that if more than ten percent of the population were found to be infected, he would have to notify the appropriate officials because it could be the sign of another mass outbreak. There is a huge list of things that would happen if that were the case, including some major restructuring of how the shelter would be set up and run. I don't know about you, but I'm pretty positive that way more than ten percent were declined entrance. I would guestimate it to be closer to thirty percent. I know too, that not everyone sent away was infected. I didn't see one person get sick. I doubt it was the shots that we took that kept us healthy. Dr. Hastings obviously didn't follow the protocol at all."

"Wow," I murmur and so does everyone else. They've all gathered around to hear these new details about Dr. Hastings. "What's truly sad is that none of this surprises me much."

"Yeah, Dr. Hastings was a very bad man," Claire says.

"At least we know that the entire U.S. government isn't corrupt. They weren't a part of the craziness that occurred here," Marya says.

"But that doesn't explain the military. If the government doesn't have anything to do with what happened here, then why did they come? Why did they take everyone away to who knows where?" Alec asks.

"That's a good question." I sigh. I'm tired of good questions. I want answers.

Connor had been sifting through more papers and he holds up one that I hadn't seen yet. "Look at this. It's some type of diagram of a machine." Tony takes it from Connor, who huffs in response but just picks up another paper from the pile.

I watch Tony as his eyes dart back and forth, devouring the words at super-human speed. He looks back up at me. "This looks like a hand written manual for the machine that somehow disables our powers. Looking at the date here, it looks like this was created four years ago."

"Meaning, he already had a backup plan for what he would do if all heck broke lose when he unleashed his super shots," I say.

"Yes, and it also looks like there is another device here that looks like the one Zack used to disarm the Reapers." Tony holds up the manual so we can see the sketch of the handheld remote that kept the Reapers down.

"Is there anything in there about how we can get around that disabling device that the military used to disable everyone's powers?" I ask.

"Not that I can find. This does explain, in scientific terms, how both devices work though." He hands the papers to me.

I leaf through them. "This isn't even in English," I say a moment later.

Tony laughs and Claire pulls the papers from my hand to look at it. "This is in English, goofy. I don't understand a lick of it, but it's in English."

Connor, Alec, and Marya all take a turns looking at it and after only a few glances, they all concur that it doesn't make a lick of sense to anyone without a Doctorate degree in Medical Science.

"Hey, look at this!" Alec says. "This looks like a deed to land. I saw the deed to this land that the house is built on and the physical address isn't far from this other one. This looks to be only a mile or so down the road."

"Interesting, especially since it was well-protected amidst all of Dr. Hasting's layers of secrecy," Tony says.

"Yeah, anything that was hidden in a secret briefcase that lay within a secret table that could only be opened by a secret code that was found in a secret-drawer compartment within a desk that is in a very secret laboratory, must be super top secret." The way Connor pronounced laboratory in a mad, European scientist-type of accent cracked me up.

"We should check this place out tomorrow," Tony says.

I yawn, the day's excitement starting to catch up with me. "Agreed." Being Sherlock Holmes isn't easy work.

"Let's call it a night," he suggests, smiling at my inner statement.

Everyone agrees with tired voices. We place all the paperwork back into the briefcase, close it, and carry it up with us. I figure that my dad will want to see this in the morning. Especially if we hope to convince him that further investigating needs to be done.

Tony and I are the last to leave the study. I can feel him close behind me as I reach up to turn off the light switch. His hand gently covers mine from behind and guides my index finger to flip the switch downward. We are plunged into darkness as the footfalls of our friends grow further and further away.

All of my other senses go into high alert and I find myself even more acutely aware of Tony than I'd ever been in the past. He slowly turns me to where we are facing each other. One hand is clasped in his and the other I reach up to place lightly on his chest, just above his heart. His heart is pounding wildly and it sends a shiver of pleasure through me. As he leans in to place his mouth on mine, I find my heart contending in a high-stakes race against his. My head goes dizzy and my knees grow weak as this kiss takes me away to places I've never been before. Just when I think I can't take any more, because if we kiss any longer it would be almost torturous to stop, Tony pulls away. He rests his forehead against mine. His breathing is heavy. We stay like this for a few minutes, until both of our hearts wind down to a simpler pace.

"I love you, Willow. Sometimes—" He seems to be having trouble vocalizing what he wants to say and I find myself listening into his thoughts. "—*Sometimes, I feel as if loving you is the single greatest and scariest thing I've ever done.*"

"*Scariest?*" I ask, bewildered.

"*Yes. You are my oxygen, Willow. If you ever left me, if anything ever happened to you…I don't think I could ever breathe again. I think I would just cease to exist right then. That is terrifying,*" he tells me.

"I won't ever leave you, Tony. I love you." I move my hand from over his heart and place it on the side of his cheek. "*If I am your oxygen, then you are my gravity, Tony. You keep me grounded. If it weren't for you holding me to this earth, I surely would have floated far, far away, filled with the pain of losing my mother. I would be drifting into space, filled with anguish. Instead, you keep me here and you fill those empty and sad places with something much bigger than words can express. You give me hope. Because if we can still find a love this powerful amidst the chaos that consumes our surroundings—then there is something to live for. There is something to fight for.*"

Without words to express his feelings, the same feelings that run amuck throughout my body, he pulls me into another kiss. This one is deeper, filled with a thirst that isn't easily quenched. Our bodies are so close that our heartbeats become one. His hands wrap around my waist and pull me even closer. I wrap my arms around his neck and revel in his touch. Then, just like before, our lips part when I think I can't take any more. "I love you," he says again.

"I love you too," I answer breathlessly.

"We should get back upstairs," he tells me but doesn't move.

"Yeah, we should."

We both stay for a few more precious moments, just relishing in the closeness of each other. Then, reluctantly, we head upstairs hand in hand.

EIGHT

I don't wake up until closer to noon.

All the excitement from the day before made for a good, high-dosage sleeping pill. When I do finally open my eyes, the sun is streaming in through the windows. I can smell freshly baked biscuits and my stomach growls. I look around and see that I must have been the last one to wake up.

I head into the kitchen and find everyone else, bright-eyed and bushy-tailed, sitting around the breakfast table.

"Good morning, sunshine," my dad says.

"Your hair funny, Wello." Sabby giggles and Lillie lets out a silly laugh.

I reach my hands up and try to smooth down my curls.

"Bedhead is hot," Tony says to me in our own secret language.

I raise an eyebrow at him and then roll my eyes jokingly before taking a seat. The biscuits are still slightly warm. I grab one and pour some honey on it. "Thank you," I tell her before taking a bite.

"No problem." Carrie smiles.

"So you want to do some exploring today?" my dad asks me.

I gulp down my bite and nod my head.

"I looked through the paperwork. That's some disturbing evidence stacked against Dr. Hastings. I am relieved to know that the government wasn't a part of this craziness," my dad says.

"Me too!" Carrie says.

"Me tree!" Sabby adds, even though he has no idea what we are talking about. He giggles again.

"You are a giggle pickle today, aren't you?" I smile wryly at him.

He and Lillie bust out in another giggle fit that has us all smiling.

"I told your dad that someone should stay here to protect the kids," Tony says.

"He was referring to me staying here." My dad arches an unamused eyebrow.

"What am I? Chopped liver?" Carrie asks. Then to demonstrate, she stands up from the table and heads to the fridge, which she persists to pick up off the ground. She doesn't lift it all the way, because she doesn't want to pull the cords from the wall. It's enough though for us to get the point. Carrie seems to be the gentle, caregiver type. She cares for the children, cooks the food, and is like the ultimate mother hen. It isn't often that we think about the power that she wields behind those neon-yellow eyes.

"You are definitely not chopped liver," my dad tells

her.

"No, Ms. W. Liver is gross! You are not chop liver," Lillie says.

"Gross!" Sabby agrees.

This makes Carrie smile. She was never very upset about the idea of needing to be protected; she just wanted to give us a reminder of what she's capable of it. "Thank you," she tells them.

"You welcome," Sabby says and Lillie agrees.

"I didn't say who should stay." Tony brings the conversation back to its origin. "I was just stating that not all of us should go. A few should stay behind with the kids."

"So you want to stay behind then?" my dad asks him.

Tony looks taken aback. "Uh, no sir. I was just thinking, what with the powers that I have, and my experience having been a fighter, that I should be a part of the party that goes."

"And since my daughter has similar experience, then she should go too?" he asks with a stern expression.

"Dad," I draw out, not knowing why he is being hard on Tony this morning. Then I feel it. He must have had a vision or something about us. He has protective papa bear emanating from him like crazy.

"He had a vision of us getting married." Tony laughs inside his head as he looks at me. *"I don't think he was ready for that. I guess he's starting to be able to see further into the future than just a few days."*

"Wow. Um, that's a little weird," I say to him, trying

not to think at all about the vision I had of Tony asking me to marry him. Hopefully, he didn't have a vision of our wedding night. I put my hand on my dad's hand. "If you want to come you can, Dad. Connor and Claire can stay."

"Hey!" Connor says, not seeming happy about the new plan.

I give him a stern look and he shuts his mouth.

My dad seems to think it through. I watch as his face flickers through an arrangement of different emotions. Finally, as if he's decided that his behavior is childish, he relents. "No, you can all go. Carrie and I will stay here. You need to go soon though. It doesn't look too far away, but I want you back before nightfall."

"Deal!" I agree. I kiss him on the cheek, scoot my chair back, and hop up from the table. "Let's do this," I say, feeling good about doing something purposeful. I know we should be finding our friends that were taken by the military, but we have no clues yet as to where they were taken. Nor do we know exactly how we can retrieve them if they are able to incapacitate our powers.

I throw on my warm clothes and then look outside. After seeing the bright landscape around the front yard, I run upstairs to search through Candy's old bedroom. I come up with a few pairs of sunglasses and excitedly bring them downstairs. Tony had rummaged through the other rooms and found a few pairs as well. I try not to think of the men they used to belong to.

With the sun out full force today, its reflection against the snow can be almost blinding. Now that we have the proper, and might I add very stylish, eye protection, we are ready to head out.

My dad and Carrie escort us to the front porch. My dad hands me a pistol, which in any other time would be an odd gesture. "Be safe," he tells me.

"I will, Dad," I assure him. I accept the pistol, check that the safety is on, and then place it in my jacket. "Love you."

"Love you too, Willow," he tells me.

I smile at him before heading off with my friends to find out what might be on this mysterious plot of land.

It doesn't take us too long to tread a mile through the partially melted snow. The entire walk passed in a deadened silence with none of us saying a single word. The only sound to be heard comes from a bird here or there and our feet plowing across the white earth. We don't even realize that we reached the address of the land until we arrive at the edge of a cliff. We saw this same drop off on the drawn map of the boundary lines. This means that we have passed through the land that Dr. Hastings owned.

"I don't see any buildings," Connor says.

"Me neither," Claire agrees.

I look around at a sea of white. The trees still dot the earth. "I guess he never used it." I don't even try to mask my disappointment. I have no idea what I hoped to find here anyway. Perhaps I thought I'd find the answer to the thousand and one questions I have.

We walk around, pacing across the acres of land, hoping to find something, anything, that can help us. We spend an hour scouring it from side to side. "Maybe he owned it and planned to use it for something in the future, but never got around to it," Marya suggests after a little while.

"Yeah, but why was he so secretive with the deed?" I ask.

She shrugs her shoulders and tosses her strawberry blonde hair over her shoulder.

"Hey! I think I found something!" Claire calls out from near a close cropping of trees.

We all run over to her. She's kicking at the ground and shoveling snow away as best she can. Connor and Alec have already started helping her.

"I felt my foot hit something hard. It might just be a tree root though," she says, looking at the trees around her.

We began to push back the remaining snow, slowly exposing a metal door meticulously made to look like the earth. The handle is the one thing that doesn't belong and makes it look out of place. The one thing Claire happened to catch her foot on. Seriously, what are the odds?

Once we've unearthed the door, Tony has us all step back while he struggles to open it. His face turns red with effort. It makes me wonder what the door is reinforced with if a man with super strength can't make it budge.

Connor comes up behind him and places his hand on his back. "I got this," he states with a smirk. Connor pokes his head through the metal door; the sight is eerie and unfitting as half of his body is plunged underground. After a handful of seconds, he pops back up.

"Dude, I was about to do that," Tony says to Connor.

"Sure you were," Connor mumbles under his breath. He turns to look at the rest of us. "It's a metal tunnel. Nothing else except that, from what I can see."

I'm about to plunge my head through to see what he's talking about, but a strange feeling stops me in my tracks. I can feel an odd sense of nervous excitement coming from the woods. I stand up and look at my friends, trying to figure out if the feeling is emanating from one of them. Tony gives me a curious look before his eyes turn black and his body tenses from having caught the feeling a moment after I did.

A throat clears from somewhere behind him and then an unfamiliar voice speaks. "Hey there."

Everyone stops dead in their tracks and look from one person to the next, everyone except Tony and me. We are already reaching for our weapons.

Claire whispers with a panic in her tone, "Who said that?"

"I mean you no harm," the voice says again.

This time we all waste no time coming together as a group and then turning into a full circle with our backs to each other—readying ourselves for any onslaught of trouble. I pull the pistol from my back pocket and point it towards the trees. There's a small rustle in the bushes and a man steps out. I immediately readjust my aim.

The good-looking man lifts his hands up in a surrendering gesture and takes a step forward into the sunlight. I survey him. He can't be too much older than we are. He's tall with a medium build. His jeans and boots are covered in snow and his black jacket looks like it has seen better days. His blonde hair is cropped close to his head and his eyes are most unusual. They are a deeply intense, blue-green that I haven't yet seen. They are shimmering with excitement at seeing us. He doesn't seem fazed at all by the gun I have trained on him. Instead, he gives me an appraising smile and I feel locked in by his gaze, by those eyes. The excited feelings rolling off this stranger are hard for me to read. I can't read his intentions at all but somehow I'm not scared and I almost feel guilty for aiming my weapon at him.

Obviously Tony can't read him either but he doesn't seem to be bogged down by the strange sense of guilt that I'm experiencing. I feel the energy leave Tony as he raises the log that was a foot in front of the man, to block his path. "Not another step," Tony shouts at him.

The log hovers in midair, making the man's interesting eyes go wide. "It's true," he whispers.

"Who are you and what do you want?" Tony demands.

Connor interjects, "Yeah, what he said." I notice though, that there isn't much conviction in Connor's voice and his stance loosens.

The grip on my gun falters slightly and I feel an untraceable tug, like its being pulled from my hand. I grip it tighter and keep the pistol aimed at the stranger, his head in my sight. I force myself to think about the facts and not think about whatever is trying to sway me to trust this stranger. The facts are that we don't know him and that he has eyes the color of the Caribbean ocean. An eye color we have yet to find!

His gaze seems to settle on me when he answers. "I'm sorry I startled you. I just wasn't sure how to approach you. I've been running from these…From these monsters for a few days now. Every time I think I've out run them or outsmarted them, they find me again. I have no idea what they want from me. When I try to ask them, they look at me with hungry eyes. I lost them a few miles southeast of here. I hadn't slowed down until I heard voices in the distance, your voices. I came to see if you could help me."

I let my pistol drop just a bit. "Are you traveling alone?" I ask him.

"Yes, yes I am," he nods. His eyes rake over me, sizing me up.

Tony steps in front of me and I have to hastily aim the gun towards the ground so as not to have it at his back. "We're going to need to search you," Tony demands.

The man thinks for a second as if he has a choice, then nods. "Okay."

Tony leaves the circle and heads towards the man. He turns him around and scoots his legs apart with his foot, just like in those cop shows I used to watch. I drop the pistol to my side as Tony searches him. The man seems unconcerned by their invasion of his privacy. Instead, he pulls his gaze away from mine and assesses the rest of us.

I don't miss the interested feelings that wash over the girls. This stranger intrigues them.

The few items Tony finds in the man's pockets are dropped on the ground during the search. It looks like a sheathed knife, wallet, a lighter, and a key ring.

Alec comes behind Tony and grabs the wallet in search of identification. "Michael Bennett, age twenty-three. Brown hair, blue eyes, 5'9", and 165 pounds," Alec says, reading his identification card aloud. He flips through the wallet some more. "Works for Atlas energy as an energy consultant. Nothing else I can tell here." Alec tosses the wallet back into the pile.

Blue eyes, I wonder. So is the color of his eyes his original color from birth? It's in this moment I realize that the one gift I rarely use could be of huge value.

I walk up to Tony, put the safety back on my gun, and slip it into my pocket. I put my hand on his shoulder as he finishes his searching procedure. "*I'm going to read his memories,*" I tell Tony.

"*Together,*" he says and grabs my hand. I notice that Tony has a swirl of silver in his eyes. He's already working to shield himself from any unforeseen threat.

I feel strangely pulled towards the man that Tony has a hold of, so I should probably do the same. A memory of Zack and his compulsion flickers in my mind and icy pinpricks cover my arms. I focus on putting up my shield as I address the man. "If you don't mind, Michael, we'd like to make explicitly sure that you mean us no harm. May we have your hand please?"

His blue-green eyes flinch almost untraceably before he hesitantly offers us his hand. I close my eyes, feeling his gaze weighing heavily on me. I do my best to ignore it as Tony and I take hold of his hand together and are instantly transported to a whirlwind of memory flashes. We go momentarily blind as we walk through his memory.

Nothing that I can see sticks out like a red flag. A non-broken home, a stay-at-home mom, private school, a high school sweetheart that died from the outbreak, a…I gasp for breath, my whole body feeling jarred as the sound of metal screeching, screams, and then an explosion fills my mind. I drop his hand and blink several times, trying to regain my sight.

"What the heck was that?" Tony asks, shaking his head in an effort to clear it.

The pain from his memory was so severe and quick that it felt like a slash, like a cut deep inside me. I run my hand over my head and through my hair, taking a few breaths. Alec has come up behind us and has his hand on both Tony's and my shoulder. Connor is training the gun Alec must have handed him, at Michael.

"What was it?" Alec asks. I can feel him sending healing into us even though it's not necessary. We didn't really get hurt—it was just a memory…Michael's poor and horrific memory.

"What did you see?" Michael asks a little too coolly.

I look up and am caught in his trance. Something tells me that he doesn't seem surprised by the fact that we just surfed through his memories. Nor does he seem surprised by our eyes, which must have gone completely white. I focus on my own healing ability, just for the sake of adding some color to my eyes. By the look on his face that turns from shock to wonder, I can tell it worked. I decide to answer his question. "A crash. An explosion."

"Oh," he says.

Tony doesn't seem too thrilled by his lackadaisical answer. "Explain," he says through gritted teeth. His hand is on his head as if he can force the sound of those screams from his mind.

"I was on the train in Baltimore," Michael says, knowing that those two words—train and Baltimore—are all we need to hear to understand.

Tony and I look to each other in horror. Claire gasps from behind us. The horrific memory makes sense now. I remember the news coverage of the accident in Baltimore. Accidents of that proportion don't happen often these days. It was only a few months prior to us entering the shelter, I think. I still remember the images of the charred and twisted eighteen-wheeler that had stalled on the tracks and derailed the passenger train in Maryland. The damage was extensive and there were very few survivors. I guess Michael was amongst the lucky ones.

I take a deep breath and look over at Michael. His eyes are filled with an intensity that only a survivor's eyes can hold. An intensity that I know all too well.

"We need to try again. We need to make sure he's safe," Tony tells me.

I nod my head in agreement. Just because he's been through something tragic, doesn't mean that he's not a psychopath. Even though I have a feeling that he's not bad.

Ending ELE

I hold my hand out to Michael. His eyes widen in surprise. I guess he thought we were done. He shrugs his shoulders and places his hand in mine. Tony quickly clasps his hand over it as well and we are sucked into the memory again. The jarring crash as the train crumples in on itself from the momentum. Michael's body being thrown from his seat, his head slamming into the window as the cart he's in tumbles onto its side…The screams erupting around him and there's an explosion from somewhere in the front of the train cart. The heat is intense and then it becomes more bearable as Michael's body is dragged out of the cart by a rescuer. Then everything goes black. I hold onto his hand for several more seconds. I feel Tony's hand lift away a moment later, but I keep my hold on Michael. I try to swim through the deep, black abyss to search for other memories, with no luck. Finally, I let go.

I allow myself a few seconds to regain my composure.

"I can't see you after the accident. What are you trying to hide?" Tony says in a stern voice with little feeling, while placing his other hand near his back pocket.

I look at Michael with the same intensity. He's hiding something, I can tell.

"I'm not hiding anything." He looks at me when he says it.

"You are," I say through gritted teeth, trying to shake his memories away from me. "I should have seen more. There were no memories after the accident. Just… Blackness."

His blue-green eyes flash with intensity that's

locked onto me. "I was in a coma for a long time. When I awoke, I was in an abandoned hospital with sweat soaking my body. They left me behind. I can only assume from the bits and pieces that I've scrounged up that they thought I was close to death and didn't bother with bringing me into one of those shelters." He curls his fingers into his fists. I can tell by his gaze that his mind is wandering back to that moment.

"That doesn't explain where your memories went since you woke up," Tony states.

Michael looks at him as if just noticing he's there.

"Yeah, why couldn't we see when you woke up?" I ask him.

"I don't know how your powers work. I've only recently learned about powers. I had found a small group of people with your kind of gifts," he answers.

"You've found people with abilities? Where are they?" I ask.

"I don't know. I woke up one morning to find them gone. I guess they left. I'm getting tired of waking up alone." His eyes are smoldering as he says the last part.

My cheeks heat at the alternate meaning and Tony steps closer to me. "That still doesn't explain why we couldn't see your memories."

Michael looks to Tony and seems a little annoyed. "Look, my mind blanks out a lot since I've woken up. Sometimes, I forget entire spans of time. I don't know for sure but that could be affecting my memory," he offers.

I glance over at Tony to see if he's buying it. He

purses his lips in thought. "Perhaps," Tony says simply. And with that, the tension that built up in the area is gone.

Michael speaks up once more, this time looking back and forth between Tony and me. "Seriously though, why do you have so many different colors in your eyes? The people I met with abilities only had one color." He points to Tony. "And you moved that log with your mind. How do you have more than one gift?" I watch as he tries to make sense of it.

"Honestly, it's a long story to get into right now. But, yes, I have multiple powers," Tony says. I can sense a bit of mistrust still floating out there between all of us and Michael. Well, I should say everyone but Marya and Claire. They seem to be drawn to him. So noticeably that Alec and Connor are starting to feel jealous. I scoff at the strangeness of it all.

Alec extends his hand in greeting, "Nice to meet you, Michael. I'm Alec, I can heal." He puffs up his chest and I can tell that he's trying to seem bigger and cooler than Michael. The two guys shake hands and we all take turns introducing ourselves, telling him our name and ability. His introduction to Claire and Marya lingers slightly longer than the rest and both blush and giggle like schoolgirls. Connor gets a bit red in the face and repositions himself so he's standing in front of Claire.

"Down doggie," I whisper in Connor's ear. The look he gives me could kill. I still manage to give him a smirk.

When it comes time for me to introduce myself, I keep my distance, not trusting myself not to be pulled into whatever web he has Claire and Marya in. "I'm Willow," I tell him, not offering up my abilities.

This doesn't go unnoticed by Michael. He arches an eyebrow and then nods acceptingly. "Nice to meet you, Willow."

I nod but don't say anything further. We all stand there in awkward silence, unsure of where to go from here.

Michael looks behind us and notices the hatch we've unearthed. "Any clue as to what's inside?" He walks over to it and gives the handle a jiggle.

Connor interjects. "It's a tunnel of some sort—not sure where it leads or anything."

Michael cocks an eyebrow. "Let me guess, you used your 'ability' to be able to see this, while the door remained sealed."

Connor grins while collecting on the ego boost. "You can say that," he says, while brushing nonexistent dirt from his shoulder. It's not often Connor takes the limelight from his ability. While cool, it's not always the most useful.

Just then, Claire lets out a shriek and is dragged away from Connor. In an instant, Connor darts around and lunges at Claire's attacker. I see the assailant's red eyes before Connor punches him in the face and frees Claire. We hadn't even thought of the threat that obviously continued to follow Michael. The monsters with red eyes!

"Reapers!" Marya calls out and the area becomes a swarm of action and fighting.

I take out my pistol, readying myself for action. Before I have a chance to know what is going on, a

Reaper painfully tackles me from behind. I feel his ability immediately, like all my powers are being sucked clean dry. Tony plucks him off me. He sends him flying through the air and into a tree trunk several yards away. I cast a glance over Tony's shoulder and, noticing it, he whirls around and begins fighting off another assailant.

I look around for the gun I dropped and can't find it anywhere. I have no time to look for it because a female Reaper is running towards me. Her red eyes and messy black hair give her a crazed look. I lift my hand in her direction and focus on moving her with my mind. The golden haze lines my vision as she lifts up from the ground a few inches. Then a silver glint flickers around the rim of her red eyes and she smirks as she drops back down and continues charging at me. I brace myself for her attack. She throws a punch. I dodge it and counter with a kick to her stomach. I put all of my power into it and she goes flying back. She's up a second later and coming at me again. I lift my hands, ready to attack, but she stops cold. Her eyes glaze over. That's when I see the blood and at the source of it, a knife is sticking out of her chest. She attempts to lift her hand up to the wound but falls to the ground lifeless in the next second.

I stare at her in confusion until Claire materializes from her invisible state. Her eyes are wide with horror and she's shaking from what she just did. I don't know if Claire has had to kill anyone yet. My stomach twists, knowing the shock she's going through.

I don't have the time to dwell on it because her

gaze flickers to something behind me. I look over my shoulder and find a Reaper with Tony in a chokehold, his face turning purple. The Reaper's eyes are crazed and swirling with red, neon yellow, gold, and silver. I try to scream and can't find my voice. I start to run to help him but a shot rings out in the clearing, stopping everyone in their tracks—Reapers and all. The Reaper that was holding Tony has a bullet that sunk clean, square in the middle of his forehead. He slumps to the ground, releasing his hold on Tony.

There are only three Reapers left alive. They take notice and immediately begin running in the opposite direction. I watch as Michael uses my gun to shoot at the rest of the Reapers. He hits one more, but the other two were way too fast.

I crawl to where Tony lies in a heap and collapse onto his chest. I try to focus my healing abilities while my brain and body still feel scrambled with fear. A second later, I feel Alec's arms embrace the both of us. I'm immediately overcome by a sense of peace and calm and I let my body relax against Tony's.

Once I feel back to normal and am sure Tony's okay and on the road to recovery, I help Alec fix the cuts and bruises of everyone with us. No one seems to be severely injured, just shaken up. Claire is only starting to come out of her shock and now she's crying. Connor is trying to comfort her. It's been a long time since we've run into any Reapers. The fact that we've kept our guard down for this long leaves us shaken at what just took place. The reality is

Reapers are still a real threat and we need to take it more seriously from now on. It would have been stupid of us to think that all of them died back in that mountain.

I hug Claire. "Thank you, Claire. You did what you had to do. It was us or them," I tell her, knowing she needs something to hold onto. I know how hard it is to deal with the aftermath of taking a life.

She tries to nod her head as she continues to sob into Connor's chest. He shhhs her and tells her what a kick butt warrior she is. I eye him and mouth, "Not helping."

He goes back to telling her, "It's okay, you did good. It's okay."

Tony stands back up for the first time since the attack and walks immediately over to Michael, who still has my pistol in his hand. Tony offers his hand to Michael and he accepts. Tony looks him square in the eyes. "I owe you my life. Thank you."

A tear springs to my eye at the realization of what just took place. It could have been a very different outcome had Michael not been here. Tony could have very well been killed. I fall to my knees and weep into my hands. The thought of Tony ever being gone from my life is just too much for me to bear. I feel Tony wrapping me in his arms and I embrace him tightly in mine.

"I thought you were gone," I say, sobbing into his chest.

"It's okay. I'm fine, see." He holds me away from his chest by the arms. I take one look at him and start crying again. His face softens and he pulls me back into an embrace, rubbing my back reassuringly. We stay like that for a while. I clench Tony's shirt in my hands, willing myself to calm down. He helps me to my feet. I take a tissue from my pocket, wiping my face and blowing my nose.

"He snuck up on me, while I was taking out one of his friends." Tony answers the question that was on my mind. Tony is so strong and often, I can consider him invincible with all of his powers. I had wondered how that Reaper almost got the best of him. Even though the Reaper snuck up on him, I can still tell that Tony is still unsure how he was stuck in a hold that he couldn't get out of.

I nod my head in understanding. I myself was caught so off guard by the entire attack that I didn't even take out *one* Reaper.

"You don't always have to be the hero," Tony speaks to me in my head.

I give him a steely look. "I don't have to be the hero, but I don't want to be the damsel in distress either."

"Honey, I'd save you from a speeding train any day, but we both know that you are far from being a damsel in distress." He kisses me on the forehead and instantly I feel better.

I look around at the others to find Claire and Connor in an embrace as well as Alec and Marya. Michael stands off to the side, still staring down at the gun in his hand. I walk over to him and he gives the gun back to me. The barrel is still warm as I put the safety on, placing it back in my back pocket. I barely know Michael but it doesn't stop me from offering him a hug. He saved my boyfriend's life and for that, I am eternally in his debt.

"Michael, do you have anywhere to go?" I keep my arm on his out of concern and focus my energy on healing. He may not be physically wounded, but I know emotionally he could use a little healing.

Michael shakes his head. "No…"

He doesn't even need to say it—it doesn't matter. "Why don't you come with us?" I offer.

He seems harmless enough, and he did save our lives. His eyes brighten. "Are you sure?" he asks, his voice filled with hope. He looks around at the other nodding heads. His face produces a smile and I return it. "We'd be happy to have you," I add.

"Yes," says Marya. "We'd be happy to have you." Alec shoots her a look. "What?" she states.

"Should we chance the tunnel? There's no telling where it leads." While contemplating our choice, I fill in Michael on why we're here and who Dr. Hastings is. He listens intently while I talk, shaking his head at appropriate intervals.

"Evil, evil man," he responds.

"I think we should chance it. We came all this way and we found the needle in the haystack—we shouldn't waste this opportunity. Plus, I doubt we'll run into any Reapers down in the tunnel," Marya states.

She has a point. "I agree," I second.

"Let's see where it leads." Tony slips his hand into mine and squeezes it. I nestle my head under his chin.

Connor, Tony, and I help everyone through the sealed door. We drop down one by one into the tunnel.

"That's strange. This is where it must dead end…in the middle of nowhere," Claire states. It does seem strange. It's completely dark down here, not a drip of light.

Michael clicks his lighter on and shines it down the tunnel.

We discover a torch attached to the wall.

"That's pretty old school. A flashlight would have been a little more practical," Claire says.

"Yeah, but a flashlight wouldn't cater to his need for dramatics," I say. "Should we light it?" Who knows if Dr. Hastings doused it with too much lighter fluid?

"I say go for it," Alec interjects. "Unless, of course, you like walking in the pitch black."

Good point. Michael takes his lighter and holds it up to the torch. It lights right away and an eerie glow fills the tunnel. He unlatches it from the wall and takes the lead. We all walk to the left of him to avoid the smoke trail the torch makes.

We walk for a good while through the twists and turns of the tunnel. Sometimes it goes uphill, sometimes down. One time, I swear I hear running water, but I can't be sure. We talk about the Reapers along the walk. Tony explains to Michael what the Reapers do. We discuss about how they had multiple powers today. A thick blanket of fear and unease falls over us as we think about exactly how they must have gotten those powers. We walk in silence for a while after that.

After walking for nearly an hour, the tunnel becomes narrow. I begin to worry that it'll become too narrow for us all to fit, until finally it dead-ends into a ladder. Michael raises the torch upwards but it's too short to completely light the path above us.

Michael notices a holder for the torch along the wall. He places it in it so that he can climb the ladder.

Seeing the holder, I can't help but think that Dr. Hastings must have thought of everything when it came to the secret passageway.

We begin ascending the ladder and eventually end up climbing in the dark. My stomach is filled with nerves as I grasp at the rungs that I can't see above me. I can hear the click, clicking of Tony's shoes climbing. Other than the sounds and our heavy breathing, our group remains eerily quiet. The atmosphere is dank and cold as we climb further upward.

I hear a small thud and then an "Ow," from further above. I can only assume it's from Michael. He must have hit his head at the top. I look up and watch as Michael, who is in front of Tony, lights the lighter again. A two-foot area around him illuminates as he raises the lighter up to the top of his head. Sure enough, it's another door. He gropes around for the handle and finds it, twisting it open. A loud squeal lets loose as the hinges creak from non-use. A small light floods the area. Michael lifts the lid further until he is able to fold it all the way back and it rests on the surface above. He moves into the room above, using his lighter to barely light the area.

Tony is the next to climb up into the room. "What the?" Tony says, stopping at the top of the ladder.

I try to urge him to keep moving so we can get off this ladder but he's stopped cold. He shakes his head, lets out a whistling breath, and then he moves off the ladder to help me up.

I look around the room and realization dawns on me. "Dr. Hastings secret room!" I exclaim. Questions of confusion float to the surface as we try to figure out what the purpose of all this mystery is.

"He needed an escape. A no-fail way out," Connor says matter-of-factly. He was the last to ascend into the room.

It makes perfect sense. Dr. Hastings knew that what he was doing was risky. He needed an escape plan—one that would buy him time to get away if need be.

Claire finds the light switch. "Let there be light," she says as she flicks it on.

I squint as it takes a few moments for my eyes to adjust to the brightness.

Alec takes the door that we just came through and closes it back up. It closes with a thud and I am in awe when I can't see the door any longer. It completely blends in with the linoleum on the floor. I squat down and examine it. I run my hand along the floor and sure enough, I can feel the outline.

"I would have never found this door. Not in a million years," I exclaim.

A round of "Me neither," sounds throughout the

room.

"So this is that evil Hastings guy's office?" Michael asks. He's already started snooping around and shuffling through drawers.

"This is his house," Marya tells him. "Or was."

Michael looks up at her with his eyebrows raised. He looks surprised by her answer, which is a strange reaction. I can't really pinpoint why it was strange but it just was. *Didn't he only just learn about Dr. Hastings?*

"Yeah," Tony answers my question. I give him that look that says, Don't you be listening in on my thoughts, and he throws his hands up in mock surrender. *"I'm just saying he's strange. I can't pinpoint how either. Something is off about him though. It's like at times I feel like he's only showing half of himself. Plus, all you girls seem to be drawn towards him. It's a bit freaky. I can't say I like it."* He arches an eyebrow at me.

"Um, not me!" I give him a stern look, but inside I know I felt some strange moth-to-flame reaction too. *"We only met him an hour or so ago. Of course, we haven't seen all of his sides yet. All that matters right now is that he's here and he saved your life. That's enough for me to know that he's on the good side."*

Tony flinches slightly, recalling his fight with the Reaper. *"Yeah, that's true."* He doesn't seem too happy about it though. It's like Michael stole his man-card or something. *"I still don't know how that Reaper got the best of me. When he had a hold of me, I couldn't use any of my powers. It was strange."*

"There are a lot of strange things going on here, but I did see that Reaper's eyes. He had many gifts and among them, there was a silver swirl in there. That's probably why he was immune to all of your powers." Tony still doesn't seem satisfied with that but it is what it is. I shiver when I think about what that Reaper had done to get so many gifts. How many people had he killed? I don't want to think about it and thankfully, a banging door pulls me away from my thoughts.

"Freeze!" a booming voice calls from the top of the stairs.

Michael's hands go up and so do Connor's. The rest of us knowingly recognize it as my dad. "It's us, Dad!" I call up.

Claire slaps Connor's arm and he drops his hands.

"Willow?" I can hear the sound of his boots clambering against the stairs. "How did you—?" He stops mid-sentence when he sees the room and sees Michael. He raises his gun at him. "Who are you?"

Strangely enough, Marya takes a step closer to Michael and so does Claire. Almost like they are willing to take a bullet for him. This takes me by surprise. "He's okay, Dad. We ran into each other outside and he saved Tony from a Reaper."

My dad's eyes go wide. "Reapers? There are more of them?" His gun aims a bit off-kilter as he contemplates this.

I nod my head. "It was foolish to think that we got rid of all of them," I say.

My dad nods in understanding and then he looks

to Tony. "You needed saving?" A humorous twinkle shines in his eyes.

Tony sucks in his cheeks and through gritted teeth answers, "Yes, I guess I did."

My dad knows better than to ruffle a man's feathers, so he moves on to address Michael. "Who are you?" he asks. His gun is at his side now and no longer pointed at his target.

Marya and Claire relax instinctively. I give them a wide-eyed 'what the heck' look. They look a little dazed and confused. With bowed heads, they each go stand by their man.

"My name is Michael, sir. I was running from the Reapers after the people I had been holed up with disappeared on me," Michael tells my dad.

I look over at my dad, who has completely put his gun away now and has moved closer to Michael. In fact, everyone I notice now has moved closer to Michael. Everyone that is, except for Tony and me. I look over to Tony and see the silver in his eyes.

"Yes, I agree," he tells me before I can even think of it.

"Twilight-zone bizarre," I confirm inside my head to Tony.

"You say these people disappeared?" my dad asks Michael.

"Yes sir. I don't know what happened. One morning I woke up and they were gone," he says.

"Do you have any powers?" my dad asks him.

I straighten up at the question, earnest to hear the

answer.

"Not that I'm aware of, sir," Michael answers, but I sense of hint of dishonesty in his words.

"Are you sure about that?" I butt into the conversation.

Michael looks over at me with mock innocence. "Like I said. Not that I know of."

"You weren't given any shots? Immunizations?" Tony interrogates.

"No. If you recall, I awoke in the hospital with nobody around." Michael seems slightly flustered, but he quickly pulls his calm facade back over himself.

"Look, it's been a long day. Let's stop with the interrogations for a little while," Claire says.

I eye her warily. She's standing between Michael and Connor, but her body is slightly tilted towards Michael, almost like she's leaning into him. "Fine," I say.

The unusually loud sound of a rumbling stomach breaks the tension in the room. We all train our eyes on Connor, who shrugs and says, "What? I'm hungry!"

The air in the room relaxes with that. "Well, Carrie has dinner almost ready. Biscuits and soup," my dad announces. He looks to Michael. "I'm sure we have enough for one more."

Michael smiles. This I don't try to judge, as I know it's genuine. There is something strange going on with Michael, but I don't think that he has bad intentions. "Thank you, sir," he says.

"Please don't call me sir. You're making me feel old,"

my dad tells him.

"Yes sir. I mean, okay," Michael corrects himself and flashes a smile. Everyone leans in towards him for a second before turning to head up the stairs.

I shake my head, trying to figure out if I'm imagining this ridiculousness. Then I follow them up the stairs and out of the secret room. The smell of fresh-baked biscuits fills the air as we walk towards the kitchen. My stomach growls in hungry response.

"Wello!" Sabby comes bounding at me when we reach the kitchen.

"Co-co!" Lillie jumps into Connor's arms.

"Hey buddy!" I tell Sabby as he hugs my knees.

"Did you go exploring?" Sabby asks me. "Dad said you did."

"You could say that." I smile down at him.

"Who's dat?" he asks when he sees Michael just behind me.

"That's Mr. Michael," I tell him. "He helped us."

My brother doesn't waste any time letting go of me and running to hug Michael.

Michael looks down in surprise at the little boy with adorable curls that is wrapped around his legs.

"Tank you for helping my sister." Sabby beams up at him. He is still hugging onto him.

Michael leans down and says, "You're welcome. What's your name?"

Sabby leans back and stands tall to announce, "I Sabby. I jus turned five!" He holds his hand out, displaying all his fingers proudly.

"Wow, that is old!" Michael tells him.

"Not as old as you, Mr. Michael. But I a big boy, yes." He smiles widely and hugs Michael again. Lillie has come up to join him, hugging Michael's other leg.

"I'm Lillie," she tells him.

"Nice to meet you, Lillie. Nice freckles! You must have been kissed by so many angels when you were a baby," he tells her.

She beams up at him. "That's what my mommy says!" She hugs him again. I can sense her mixed emotions that range from missing her parents to being excited about this new visitor.

"All right, kids. I think it's time that you give our guest a little personal space." Carrie comes up and puts her hands on each of the kid's shoulders, redirecting them towards the table. "Take a seat. Dinner is nearly ready."

"Yes, Ms. W."

Michael holds his hand out to introduce himself to Carrie. "My name is Michael. Your food smells amazing. I can't tell you how good a hot meal sounds about now."

"Thank you. I'm Carrie Wallobee, or Ms. W. for anyone that is pint-sized." She smiles and takes Michael's hand. She leans in a tad while shaking it for an awkwardly long period of time.

Michael is the one to pull his hand away and take a polite step back. "Is there somewhere I can get washed up?" he asks.

"Yes, there is a bathroom just off the living room,"

Carrie answers. "Would you like me to take you there?"

We all stand open-mouthed. Carrie immediately realizes what she just said and blushes. "I mean," she corrects herself, "let me know if you need anything."

He tips his head back and says, "Thank you," before retreating to the restroom.

"That wasn't awkward at all," I say under my breath, close enough so that only Tony can hear me.

"You're telling me," he replies.

We all take turns washing our hands at the kitchen sink and Michael joins us a few minutes later. His face is washed and he looks excited to eat, rubbing his hands together.

"I haven't had a warm meal in a long time," Michael tells Carrie as the biscuits are passed around the table and the soup ladled out into bowls.

"I know. We're getting spoiled with Carrie being around," my dad says with a smile.

Carrie waves him off like it's nonsense.

"How did you come about this place?" Michael asks.

"I had a vision about it. I didn't realize it was Dr. Hasting's house though," Tony tells him.

"You had a vision?" Michael asks, his eyebrows furrowed.

"Yes, sometimes we can see stuff that happens in the future. Little glimpses," I answer for Tony. "My dad has them as well."

"That's really cool," Michael says, looking over at my dad. He seems like he is just noticing the strange copper shade for the first time.

"Yeah, we lucked out to find a place with electricity. Leave it to that jerk to be the only house with running power and water!" Connor says with half a biscuit in his mouth.

The remainder of the dinner conversation is filled with us catching Michael up on all that has happened since we left the shelter. We tell him about our run in with Dr. Hastings and Zack, as well as our friends being taken by the military. I get a strange sensation when we talk about the military part and I wonder if that might be who took his friends away too.

Michael asks if he can stay with us a while longer. My dad tells him that he can stay however long he needs. We aren't the kind of people who would turn someone out in times like this. After dinner, we settle in for bed. With little energy left from the crazy day we've had, we all find ourselves falling asleep rather easily.

NINE

The sound of someone moving about in the room wakes me up.

I wrestle my sleep-filled eyes open and try to look around in the dark. I make out a shape near the far side of the room. I sit up quietly as not to disturb Tony or Claire, who lay close to where I am, and I tiptoe over.

The pale light of the moon is enough for me to make out Michael working his shoes on near the front door. He looks up when he sees me approach. I don't know if it's because I'm tired, but he doesn't seem surprised to see me standing there.

"What are you doing?" I ask in a hushed whisper.

"I need to show you something," he whispers back.

I step closer, intrigued and pulled to him.

"Put on your shoes and coat," he tells me.

I comply, not thinking twice about where we are going. A strange man, alone in the dark woods, all of a sudden doesn't feel strange at all. We stealthily slip down the hall a moment later. I expected that we would be going outside, but instead, we head in the direction of Dr. Hastings's study. We quietly open the path to the secret room. Michael finds a battery-operated lamp and works to open up the other secret passageway in the floor. I climb in after him. It isn't until we've closed the door and are lit in lamplight that we talk again.

"Where are we going?" I ask him, a little out of breath as I descend on the ladder above him.

"I couldn't sleep because I kept thinking about what you said about the military taking your friends. I feel like I've seen something that could be their operation. It wasn't far from here, but there is a city of tents set up with a barbed-wire fence surrounding it," he tells me as we continue to climb down.

He hits the ground first and then reaches up to help me off the ladder. His hands are on my sides as he helps to set me on the ground. A strange sensation pangs through me. I turn and find myself standing only an inch or so apart from him, yet something makes me want to stand closer. I lean into him, my ear is pressed up against his chest and I can hear his nervous heartbeat. I feel glued, stuck, yet I can't bring myself to move. My thoughts are nowhere to be found until he clears his throat lightly.

I startle and try to pull myself away. It's as if a thousand pounds are pushing me into him though. I have to call on my power of strength to merely step back a foot from him. The daze washes away and I'm left feeling extremely awkward. *What in the world was that?* I think to myself. I look up at him blushing. Thankfully, it's quite dark in here.

He smiles at me with pearly white teeth as if nothing happened. I take another step back because I want so badly to lean into him again but I know that isn't right. I'm not attracted to this man. I mean, sure he looks like James Bond and hasn't been hit by the ugly stick or anything, but this isn't attraction that I feel. I love Tony and no other guy does what Tony does for me. This is different though. It's like a force is pushing me to Michael and I'm drawn like a helpless moth…He's a flame, a flickering…I step forward…

I shake my head again and take another two steps back. *Get it together!* I tell myself. My body still feels exhausted from the previous day and spending the energy to stay apart from Michael leaves me even more spent.

He tries to act like he hasn't noticed my strange behavior. He turns and starts walking down the path. I follow him like a lost puppy, still unsure what is up with my strange behavior.

We walk in silence the whole way. I end up walking beside Michael after a few minutes. Every once in a while, I lean in so far towards him that our arms brush each other's and I nearly get my foot stepped on by his because I'm moving into his walking space. He doesn't say anything though. It's almost like this is normal for him.

When we come to the end of the tunnel, Michael fumbles with the lock. It's rusted and unwavering. I have to spend a few moments clearing the hazy fog in my brain to be able to focus on the gift I got from Connor. After a few unsuccessful tries, I eventually manage to get us out into the frosty night. A light dusting of snow is falling softly from the sky.

The cold air does a lot to wake me up. Michael

starts moving towards the trees. I zip my jacket up and begin following him. The longer we remain outside, the clearer my mind becomes.

We don't walk too far before Michael says, "It's only down past that ridge." He stops mid-step and I pummel into his back. I have to exert nearly all of my energy to break myself apart from him again. I follow his fingertip as he points somewhere beyond the trees. I focus my eyes a little better and eventually make out the glowing haze of lights a few miles off in the distance. "Let's go check it out."

I stop. The not-rightness of the situation washes over me. Instinctively, I make to protect myself. I know my eyes must be silver because when Michael looks back at me, expecting me to follow him, he startles. The magnetic pull I had to him has been severed and now I'm left feeling very unsettled with this whole situation.

"Why didn't you wait until everyone else woke up, Michael?" I ask, taking a step back. My heart starts beating frantically, notifying me that something isn't right.

His eyebrows furrow and he gives me his best look of shock. I try to read his thoughts but they are blank. His feelings, I can read though. There is a hint of nervousness and almost like a scant feeling of second-guessing himself. Other than that, I don't get any malicious intent coming from him, so I relax slightly.

"I don't know what you mean, Willow," he says carefully. "Why are your eyes silver?" he asks me.

I wave off his question. He doesn't need to know about this particular gift. "My question was clear, Michael.

Why did you not wait until we were all awake? Why take only me?"

I'm brought off balance as my mind is drawn into another place. I vaguely feel myself hit the ground and my eyes go dark before the hazy vision takes over. The sun is beginning to rise and I'm back in the Hastings's living room. No pillows or blankets are lying out and I wonder why everyone woke up so early. The sky is still dark as night. Then the glass shatters. A spraying of bullets flies into the room. I dive to duck for cover. Michael is there. He's jumped on top of me to shield me. I feel his body jerk back as a bullet hits his shoulder. He groans. I quickly focus my healing on him.

"We have to move!" I tell him. He grunts and we start crawling towards the study.

I turn us invisible as the door crashes down in the living room. Orders and footsteps fill the silent air. My heart races, wondering where my family is. I enter the study and as I close the door to the room, my eyes lock onto a figure that is running in my direction. Mr. Blake! He can see me! He must have the same gift Candy did. I never questioned what his original power was before he injected himself with my blood.

"I will get you, Willow!" he yells as I slam the door.

Using my power of strength, I push a metal cabinet in front of the door. I throw a chair through the window, hoping to divert their attention to where I'm really headed. Then I pull Michael with me through the secret passage, into Dr. Hastings room, and down into the tunnel beneath the floor.

※

"Willow!" I hear my name being called in the distance. A stinging pain hits my cheek. "Willow, are you okay?" I can hear the voice a little closer now. It's a man. "Willow," he asks worriedly. My cheek is hit again and I snap my eyes open.

Michael is leaning over me. His face a mask of concern. I gasp as I look up into the pre-dawn sky. "We have to go back now!"

Michael looks relieved that I'm okay but not happy with my order. "No, we need to go check out the base," he tries to urge me.

I sit up carefully and lean into him. I'm about to say okay, but then the vision comes back to my mind. I shoot my shield up and the strange pull is released again. "No! I have to go back now! They are coming for my family. I have to get back there," I yell at Michael.

His eyes widen and a look of pure conflict crosses his face. He looks towards the camp and back at me a few times. His look is torn. I don't waste any time grabbing his hand. I'm going to have to utilize two abilities if I have any chance at getting back to the house in good time. His face contorts a little as he watches my eyes swirl with silver and yellow.

"We're going to run, Michael. We're going to run very fast." Before he has a chance to question my motives, I whisk us off with ample speed in the direction of the house. I don't bother utilizing the tunnel. The open air keeps me grounded and focused. I hear a yelp from Michael as his legs struggle to keep up with mine. He puts his hand up to guard his face as if he's going to run into low-lying tree branches.

"Michael," I say to him calmly. "Put your hand down. I'm not going to let you hurt yourself."

His arm shakes just a little as he lowers it—his eyes wide with fear. The trees whip by us as I lead us through the woods and back to the house. I don't go as fast as I can, for fear Michael may pass out. I could take him piggyback style but it doesn't seem very ladylike.

We make it back to the house in half the time. I slow our run as we approach. The house is just as we left it. Crickets are chirping in the background and I breathe a sigh of relief—we still have time. I utilize Connor's gift again and get us through the locked front door.

I tiptoe over to where everyone is sleeping—only to find everyone gone. My breath catches in my throat and I realize my worst nightmare is coming true. I turn towards Michael and at the same time, the picturesque window behind us is shattered into a million pieces. Guns begin to fire in all directions as Michael leaps on top of me. He lets out a grunt as we land on the floor. He grabs his arm in pain and I see the blood pooling from his hand.

Realizing my vision is coming true, I know the door is about to come crashing in. Healing will have to wait. I grab his good arm and pull him with me. We crawl on all fours to avoid being hit by more flying bullets. As soon as we reach the hallway, the door has officially been blown in. I instinctively turn us invisible as we crawl the rest of the way to Dr. Hastings's secret room. The house is a sea of commotion as dozens of black clad men armed enter the house.

We crawl through the bookcase and come out on the other side. Michael collapses on the floor, writhing in pain. He grips his shoulder tightly where the blood seeps through his fingers.

I turn his face towards me with my hands, making him look at me and not the floor. "You are going to be okay. I'm going to fix it—just sit still."

Michael's face is one of confusion as I place my hands on his shoulders and focus on my healing energies. Within a few moments, he stops groaning. The bullet falls into his hand as it's pushed from his arm. He stares at it in disbelief.

The sound of screaming orders and furniture being overturned sounds off in the adjacent room. As I wipe Michael's blood off my hands by rubbing them against the carpet, a thought invades my mind. It's a horrific one. I look up swiftly at Michael, who still sits in stunned silence. "We have to find everyone. What if they're hurt? They may still be in there!" I leave Michael on the floor and rush back over to the wall.

Just as I'm about to go through it, he tugs me back. "Stop!" he demands of me.

"Are you insane?" I whisper harshly. "My family and friends are in there. They may even be dead!" Tears rush to my eyes and cloud my vision. My logical thinking is

Ending ELE

gone and all I can think about is the need to be near them, regardless of what may be happening on the other side of this wall.

Michael looks at me sternly. "No, Willow! You can't help them, but you can help yourself. It's what they would want."

I look at him incredulously. "How the heck would you know what they want? *You* don't even know me or my family!" He flinches ever so slightly at my words.

I'm about to use my strength to break free from his grasp when a calming sensation runs through me. I can't tell if it's from Michael or what but I invite it in. Something deep down is telling me to go—to get to safety. I nod my head at Michael and he understands.

We rush to the door in the floor and pry it open. With my energy spent from emotions and from healing Michael, I can barely grab hold of any of my abilities, let alone use them. I get on the ladder first and Michael follows closely behind, closing the latch behind him. We hasten our descent, taking the rungs one by one. When I reach the bottom, I let go of the rung and drop to the floor. A few seconds later, Michael drops down next to me. I can hear the distant sound of feet thumping in the study above us. It leaves me with a sick churning in my stomach.

I hear Michael fiddling with his lighter as he attempts to light our path. Neither of us took the time to grab the torch in our quick getaway. I see the first spark of the lighter and then a small glow emanates from his hand. He shines the lighter in front of us and I almost scream. My family and friend's faces stare back at me…and so does a gun pointed between my eyes.

My dad lets out a heavy exhale and drops the gun to his side. "Willow! Thank God you're okay." He makes a gesture with his eyes upwards, saying a quick thanks to the Man upstairs.

I look past my dad to Marya and Alec. My heart starts racing as horrible possibilities cross my mind. "Where are they? We have to go back to get them!" My voice chokes on the last part when images of my baby brother, Tony, and everyone else still in that house come flooding in. I turn quickly to run back in that direction but my dad grabs my arm.

"They're safe, Willow. Carrie, Connor, and Claire kept going in the tunnel with both of the kids. Connor is leading them to safety," my dad tells me.

"What about Tony?" I ask, still shaking from the adrenaline that's coursing through my veins.

"He is trying to find you. Both Tony and I had the vision in our sleep. We woke up and found both Michael and you missing. Then when we realized that we both saw the same vision, we quickly got everyone down here. Tony went out to find you. I'm not sure where he is. He saw your coat missing, so I'm sure he's outside somewhere," my dad says, his relief turning to worry when he sees my expression. I don't even have to say anything. He quickly adds, "Then we are coming with you."

"It's not safe, Dad," I tell him.

"Nothing is safe anymore, honey. We're going with

you anyway." He pulls me into a hug with his arm that's not holding the gun.

"He left through the front door but I think his plan was to double back above ground, towards where this tunnel leads out," Alec informs me.

"Okay, let's get a move on." I don't wait for their replies. I barrel forward through the tunnel. I want badly to use my speed but I also don't want to leave my father and friends behind. Not when there is a crazy madman and his blood-hungry loons on our tails.

We reach the end of the tunnel several minutes later. I help everyone out and into the freezing dawn. Snow is falling heavier now and while the sun is rising, heavy grey clouds are blotting it out. Part of me is grateful for the added protection that the snow provides and another part realizes that it will make it harder for me to find Tony or vice-versa.

I look around to see Connor running out from behind a grouping of trees. Then I see Sabby's head peeking around the corner and he comes barreling for me.

"Wello!" he yells before he clasps his hands over his mouth with wide eyes. "I sowry. I suppose to be quiet as a mouse," he whispers and tiptoes the last few steps into my arms.

"I'm just glad you're okay. I love you," I say in a whisper. I look over at Connor. "Have you seen Tony?" The concern is clearly etched on my face.

"Not yet," Connor answers sullenly.

I swallow, trying to stave off the nausea that ensues

with my panic. *"Tony!"* I try to yell inside my head several times. We can't scream aloud. We have no idea how far away the enemy is.

"You need to take them to safety," my dad tells Connor.

"Where should I go?" Connor asks. None of us are completely sure of our surrounding area. We should have staked this place out better.

"Head north east," Michael tells him. "You should be able to find shelter along the way."

"No!" I stare at Michael incredulously. "We have no idea where those lights are coming from. You can't send them that way."

Michael shakes his head and a look of pure confusion crosses his features. Almost as if he can't comprehend why I would be worried about heading in that direction or sending my family there. "I wouldn't send them that way if I didn't think it was safe," he tells me. I bite my lip, trying to figure out if I believe him.

"You saw lights?" my dad asks, interrupting my thoughts.

I nod my head and Michael says "Yes, sir," at the same time.

"How far away?" Claire asks. Lillie is hugging her leg and Carrie's leg with the other arm.

"Several miles but still!" I retort.

"We could just head in the direction and find a suitable place to take cover," Connor tells me.

I take a deep breath. No visions, signs, or feelings

are alarming me that this is a bad move, so finally I relent. "Fine—but, be safe! Make sure to keep a lookout for us."

"We will," he tells me.

Claire gives me a hug. "You be safe too, Willow."

"Always." I give her a wry grin. I look over at Michael and consider sending him with the others, but I don't. I can't tell if I trust this man just yet and I'd rather have him close to me and not with my little brother.

As Connor, Claire, Carrie and the kids run off, I begin frantically calling for Tony again in my head. *"Tony!"* I need him to hear me.

Please let the vision be true, I think to myself. *He has to be okay. He's going to ask me to marry him…* My thoughts trail off as I try to make a connection with Tony.

Alec, Marya, Michael, and my dad stand with me, not sure about what to do next. I cock my head to the side and they follow me into the brush. At least this way we won't be in the middle of a field and vulnerable to an attack.

Think Willow, think. Alec, Marya, and my dad start leaning in towards me. It's kind of creepy and they're definitely invading my personal space. I raise my hand at them. "Give me a little room, please," I whisper. It's like they didn't even realize they were leaning towards me as they blush and look away. *Okay, that was weird.* Michael crouches about two yards in front of us, looking at us all huddled together awkwardly.

I give him a stare that says, *You better not start too.* Thankfully, he obliges and keeps his distance.

We stay huddled together for what seems like

forever, Michael taking point. As the minutes tick by and with no sign of Tony, nervousness courses through my veins like tiny steam engines. I try to fight the anxiety but find it hard to just sit here and do nothing.

"Psst," I say, trying to get Michael's attention. He stealthily bridges the gap between us. Alec, Marya, and my dad have again allowed themselves to become plastered against my side. I kindly try to push them away so I can get some air again. Thankfully, Michael doesn't mention it.

"I can't stand to wait here any longer," I whisper to the group. I feel like ants are crawling all over my skin. I'm about to come unglued. Not being able to communicate with Tony or know if he's okay has my stomach in knots. Michael nods in understanding.

Michael pipes up into the silence. "We have to be smart about this. We can't let our emotions get the better of us."

I nod my head. The simple act of standing and running in the direction of the house full force wouldn't be a good idea for any of us. Still…don't think that thought hasn't crossed my mind. I rub my chin, trying to think.

"I think we need to split up," I say. "We'll cover more ground that way. I know it isn't ideal but I can't just sit here and hope Tony crosses our path."

"I agree," my dad says. The others nod their heads in affirmation.

"I'll take Michael with me and you three stay together." I can't mention that even though Michael saved Tony's life, I still don't trust him completely…Well, at least not enough to leave him alone with one of my friends or family. His intentions are about as clear as muddy water to me. Thankfully, the others agree.

"We'll go to the left, as far as the river, and stake out that area. You three go to the right. With any luck, one of us will find Tony along the way. We can meet back at the river below the cave that we stayed in before we found the Hastings' house." I shiver at the name but continue. "We need to be especially careful as we stake out the house. There's no doubt that these guys will have left a surveillance team in the hopes that we decide to come back."

I look over at Michael and see the agreement in his eyes. Marya is almost in my lap and I not so kindly push her away arm's length. She begins to lean towards Michael, making Alec slightly irritated. Removing Michael from the equation might be a good idea, considering the murderous look on Alec's face right now.

I pull my dad in for a hug. "Please be careful," I whisper, hugging him tight.

He pats my back, a soothing and comforting gesture. "I will," he whispers back. He pulls me back at an arm's length and looks me in the eyes. "Don't do anything to risk your life, Willow. And I mean it. I know you love him, but we need you too," he says in his stern, fatherly voice.

I nod my head that I heard him…I just can't make that kind of promise though. I would do anything to keep Tony safe. But, right now, my dad doesn't need to know that.

We all say our goodbyes and part ways. I watch as their figures fade into the early dawn light before Michael and I leave. We comb the area, looking for Tony. I bite my nails as we walk, a gesture of nervousness I thought I had outgrown.

"You know, biting your nails is not a very good habit," Michael says, pointing out the obvious.

I give him a look that says, *Leave me alone.* He chuckles and shakes his head but keeps his comments to himself.

"He's obviously not around here. We are going to need to get closer to the house," I tell him, feeling frustrated after walking circles around the perimeter of Dr. Hastings's secret exit for over twenty minutes.

"I guess we have no choice then." He doesn't look happy about it, but he straightens his shoulders and nods his head in a 'move out' kind of way.

We don't talk much throughout the mile walk there. Mostly because we don't want to give away our position but also because we have nothing to say to each other.

The knots in my stomach begin tightening as we near the house slowly and carefully. I try not to think about all that is at stake here.

Michael starts moving to higher ground above the house and I follow his lead. We'd have a better vantage point of the area from up there. We make our way to the top of a small hill and look down. We can see the home about a quarter mile away.

"We should go invisible and make our way closer

to the house," I say to Michael, breaking our silence. "My only worry is they have someone stationed at the house with light blue eyes, able to see through my abilities."

Michael scratches his chin, contemplating this. He nods and I grab his hand, noticing how *not* like Tony's his hand is. We take one last look down the hill and then we go invisible.

Stealthily, we make our way down towards the house. I notice Michael looking down every now and again, obviously surprised to not see the rest of his body. It looks somewhat silly for someone like me, who can see him clear as day. He examines his other hand, turning it this way and that.

The sweat in our hands meld together and I can only hope that if Tony sees us first that he understands why I'm holding onto Michael's hand. With the house about a hundred yards ahead of us, we crouch down behind a fallen tree.

I bite my lip, trying to sense if someone is near us. I let go of Michael's hand now that we are safely out of view.

"I don't see anyone," I whisper to him. I want to try to make my way back inside the house. Perhaps Tony is still in there.

Michael pulls out a pair of binoculars from his backpack. He scans the area, looking for anything suspicious. I do the same minus the binoculars. I find a small raccoon wandering over by the house and I watch as it leads her babies over the forest floor, foraging for food.

Michael taps me on my arm, hands me the

binoculars, and points towards something. I put them up to my eyes and it doesn't take me long to register a man. I am shocked that Michael even found him.

The man is covered from head to toe in a Ghillie suit. The only way I can notice him is when he goes to move the suit aside to take a sip of his water. I refocus the binoculars so I can see him better. I want to see what color his eyes are. After his large swig of water, the man sets the bottle down next to him on the floor. He takes a rag and uses it to wipe the sweat off his brow. That's when I catch a glimpse of his eyes.

"Light blue," I whisper to Michael as I keep a close watch on his actions.

I zoom back out and watch the man readjust the Ghillie suit back into place. I zoom out a bit when I see his suit shake as he gets up off the ground.

The raccoon had gotten closer to the man and must have not sensed him stationed near the house. The raccoon stops as the man stands up. Her babies have stopped as well and are clustered around their mother. The man reaches his hand out, trying to shoo away the raccoon, frantically waving his hands around.

It looks strange though. I know there is a man there, but all it looks like is leaves fluttering in the wind. One of the babies, I guess not sensing any danger, starts walking in the direction of the man. The man seems to be trying to get out of the suit as he wildly waves his arms and legs around. The little baby raccoon trips over something. I can't find the source of what it must have tripped over,

Ending ELE

guessing it must have stumbled on a branch along the forest floor. The mama raccoon rears up on her back legs, ready to protect her baby. The man, not caring that he's still in the suit, begins running wildly away from the house and the raccoon.

"What the…?" I whisper but am cut off when Michael slams me to the ground, knocking the binoculars from my hands. I opened my mouth to protest when an explosion rings out through the trees. Starbursts shoot across my closed eyelids, my head is pounding against a deafened silence, and I can feel the heat immediately lick at my skin. I lie in the same position, seemingly unable to move. After what seems to be several minutes, in a mess of confusion, I turn my head toward the direction of the house. All I can see is a massive ball of flames as the house burns wildly in the cold, morning air.

I don't register Michael's absence when I first I sit up. My mind is still working to focus beyond the disorientation and confusion that the explosion caused. The ringing in my ears intensifies as my hearing ability increases. The remaining snow around me is melting, quickly turning to water and soaking into the ground. I begin to sweat underneath my clothes, the heat from the flames becoming overwhelming. I need to get out of here. I look around at my surroundings and can't spot Michael anywhere.

Without warning, someone behind me puts their hand over my mouth. I go to scream but nothing comes out. I writhe and thrash around, trying to escape for my life. There is no doubt in my mind that the man in the

Ghillie suit has found me. Did they set off the explosion to throw me off guard? Fighting with all I am worth, using every last ounce of strength, I try to struggle loose, but to no avail.

A small voice begins to speak inside my head. *"Willow, Willow!"* I recognize Tony's voice filter through my mind.

"Tony!" I scream back. He can help me. I just need to fight this man off until Tony can get to me. I continue to fight harder against my assailant, promising myself to never give up. I'm flipped over with an ease that comes from someone with a good deal of strength. It gives me a new advantage to fight face to face with my attacker. I finally get a good look at his face and my hands stop hitting and fighting back.

I wrap my arms around Tony. I was so scared I hadn't even considered it was him behind me. Tears spill down my cheeks as I draw in his comforting embrace. My mind does not want to believe it is really him. I pull him back so I can see his face…that beautiful face. I put my hand to his cheek, running it down his stubble.

"It's really you…" I say to him in my mind.

He nods. *"I'm fine, Willow. Everything is going to be okay."*

Still relishing the fact that Tony is okay, a thought strikes my mind. *Michael. Where is Michael?* I have no idea where he would have disappeared.

Tony, having sensed my thoughts, pulls me at arm's length, looking around the area. The flames still lick the sides of the house but have diminished in intensity.

"We can't wait for Michael," Tony says to me. "He'll be fine. I have to get you out of here though…somewhere safe. We're completely exposed out here."

I feel guilty leaving without Michael but Tony has a point. I don't know Michael that well, but if I had to bet, he'll be fine out in the woods by himself. His survival skills are more than ample. Also, he knows where to meet us since all five of us set up the location at the cave to meet back up at. That thought comforts me a little. "Okay then, we need to meet my dad, Alec, and Marya by the river. That's our rally point."

Tony nods in agreement. I wobble a bit when we get moving again, but Tony's healing ability filters through me, helping to steady me. He takes the lead as usual and I follow him quietly away from the burning remains of the Hastings's house.

"Where did the others go?" Tony asks as we run quietly through the forest, staying within the shadows of the trees.

"They took the kids out towards some lights that Michael saw not too far away from here. We think it may be the military camp," I tell him.

"What? Why didn't I know about this?" he asks without stopping.

My breathing is labored as we pick up speed. "He just showed it to me this morning. They aren't going to go near the lights, just in that direction." Tony's free hand clenches into a fist. I can feel the jealousy and mistrust—towards Michael, not me—rolling off him. I do my best to brush it off, knowing that I need to let him blow off some of this steam before we talk about my disappearing into the night with Michael. *"They are supposed to find a safe place to wait for us."*

The sound of a gunshot rings out in the air behind us. I drop to the ground automatically, even though it came from back near the burning house. Nowhere near us. My blood runs ice cold as realization hits me. "Michael." I whisper out loud. I genuinely hope he's okay.

"We don't know that. We need to keep moving." Tony pulls me up and we run faster towards the river.

It has to be Michael. Guilt tries to creep in as I think of my dad, Alec, and Marya. It has to be Michael, not one of them.

Tony grabs my hand and squeezes it. All without missing a step, he tells me, *"Don't think about it, Willow. If it was Michael, we don't know if he was on the giving or receiving end of that gunshot. We just need to get to the rally point and wait for him and the others."*

Another startling realization hits me. *"He won't make it to the rally point."*

"Why not?" Tony asks.

I duck under a low-lying branch and sidestep a large rock. *"Because I told them to meet us at the river beneath the cave we stayed in. Michael doesn't know which cave we stayed in."* I don't have proof that there are more caves in the general area, even though that's usually the case. I begin to wonder why he didn't question me about it…My explanation was very nondescript in the first place, especially for someone like Michael, who hadn't been there before.

"*Well crap,*" Tony says, although I can tell he isn't too concerned about finding Michael. I think that statement was more for my sake than anything.

"*If he's smart, he'll double back and head toward the lights. He knows we are bound to try and meet up with the others soon.*" The sound of the waterfall grows closer as we move at lightning fast speeds in its direction.

"*We can't afford to wait around for him too long. If those lights are from the military camp, we need to put some distance between ourselves and it,*" Tony says as the waterfall comes into view.

"*We need to save the others. We have to investigate—find out where those lights are coming from.*" I stop behind a large tree and turn to look at Tony. I'm surprised that he wants to keep running when we don't know if the others are safe.

His neon-yellow eyes flash with intensity. "*What do you expect, Willow? For us to go rushing in there and demand that the army of soldiers just give up their hostages?*"

"*We don't know that they are hostages,*" I say back, while giving him a snarly look. My reasoning makes no sense though. Why would they have taken everyone in? *Not* to make new friends. I don't know though. I have a strange feeling that the people who took them aren't planning to harm them. After all, there wasn't a single casualty left behind. If they intended to harm them, they would have used serious force. "*Look, I'm not saying that we rush in there without a plan. I'm saying that we need to investigate the camp. We don't even know if it's a military camp. That could be Blake's men."* I surely hope not though. From what I could see, the camp was huge. If Blake has that much backing behind his vicious schemes, then we are in a legion of trouble.

The sound of footsteps makes us both go still. Tony raises his hand to my mouth and instantly we both go invisible. The footsteps near and I realize it's more than one set of feet trampling through the snow. The tree that we are hiding behind begins to shake. Tony and I dive to the side as it starts lifting from the ground, uprooting the roots.

"Willow!" my dad calls in a loud whisper.

The tree drops back in place as my dad, Alec, and Marya come into view. Marya looks relieved and out of breath from lifting such a large object with her mind.

"Dad." I run to hug him, so relieved to have him safe.

"I see you found your man," he whispers into my hair before releasing me. I chuckle at his words.

"Actually, he found me," I tell him, releasing the hug.

"We were so worried about you. We heard the explosion and saw the smoke," Marya tells us.

"I wanted to check it out, to make sure you were okay, but Alec has a good head on his shoulders. He reminded us that Blake's men could have set a trap. I agreed to check here first before going to investigate," my dad tells me.

"I'm glad you listened to Alec. We heard a gunshot

as we were running this way. I'm not sure if Michael made it. He disappeared shortly after the explosion and I couldn't find him," I report to them.

"We better get going to find the others," Tony recommends. "How far off were the lights, Willow?"

"It's a few miles from Hastings's secret exit," I reply. Tony nods his head. "Let's move out then."

It takes us under an hour to make it to the point just beyond the secret exit. I see the ridge that Michael pointed out early this morning. Just beyond it, somewhere in the distance, is the base camp of the military. At least we are hoping it's the military and not Blake's posse.

Getting here was the easy part. Now we have to find the others. My stomach is growling loudly from hunger. Tony hands me half a protein bar with a reassuring smile.

I feel on edge. I don't like being separated from my little brother or my friends. I will feel much better when I know everyone is okay. We make our way towards the ridge. It was easier to make out the lights of the camp when it was dark. Now, during the daylight that is slowly starting to wane away, it's hard to find the spot in the distance.

I squint my eyes, searching for it. The ridge slopes down into a valley of snowcapped treetops for as far as I can see. Nothing sticks out to me. The lights were a few miles away from this point when I saw them. I point to Tony in the general direction that I recall Michael pointing. "It's somewhere out that way."

"It's going to be hard to make it out during the daylight if it's that far away. Do you think the others would have stuck around up here, or do you think they made their way down into the valley?" Tony asks aloud. It seems to me like a rhetorical question.

"It's hard to say. We weren't specific on where they were to hide. We just asked them to bunker down somewhere safe and to keep an eye out for us," I answer. I try to open myself up in hopes that I can sense them nearby. I give up a few seconds later with a small feeling of defeat.

"We should probably scour this area up here first, and then make our way down if we don't find them," Alec suggests.

"Sounds like a plan to me." Tony pats him on the back.

We split up to search the perimeter. Marya and Alec take one direction and my dad, Tony, and I take the other. An hour later, we meet back at the ridge with no sign of the others.

"Let's head down then," I say as I take the lead. Thankfully, the slope downwards isn't steep. We're able to work our way down easily and quickly.

When we make it back under the canopy of trees that seem thicker than they were up above, we begin looking around again. My stomach feels unsettled and Tony, having sensed my anxiety, squeezes my hand. I've been trying not to think of the many dangers out here. I can't help it though. They could run into Reapers, Blake's men, the military, a bear…Really, the list is endless.

"Carrie could totally take a bear," Tony says trying to be helpful.

"Yeah, she totally could." I give him a half-smile and continue looking around us. A small amount of snow begins falling from the sky, blanketing the ground in a new layer of white.

"Willow," Marya calls from behind me.

I turn around to see her with a hand on my dad's shoulder. His face is blank as he looks at nothing in particular. A moment later, the fog clears from his expression and he looks up with a wondering smile.

Hope rises in me. "Did you see them?"

He nods his head, still smirking. "Yes, they aren't too far from here. Connor found a tree house."

"A tree house?" Alec asks.

"Yes, or it could be a hunting blind. I couldn't tell. All I know is that there isn't much to it, but it's keeping them out of the way," he answers.

"Do you know where it is?" Marya asks.

"It's near a small creek. Where the creek is, I have no idea. We must find them soon though, since it was still daylight in my vision." My dad pats her hand, which was still on his shoulder.

She smiles and drops her hand. She was worried about my dad and that means she cares for him. I like that.

"Good. They have the food," Alec jokes.

"Let's keep heading in this direction then," Tony says since we don't have a better plan.

We keep moving forward. Every once in a while, we stop and fan out to search the area around us and then meet back in the middle again. It's on one of those searches that Marya and Alec report that they found the creek.

"It was covered in snow, making it hard to see, but it's definitely a creek," she tells us as we follow them.

The creek is small but keeps going on for as far as we can see. We follow the bank a short ways before we hear them.

"Wello!" Sabby calls out to me.

I turn around to look behind me. When I hear his giggles, I look up to see my brother above us in the tree house. His little face is smiling at me from its cut-out window. Connor and Claire are peeking out behind him. The place is very well camouflaged. If Sabby hadn't called out, I never would have noticed it.

We move towards the tree. "How do we get up?" Tony calls up.

A second later, a hatch opens above us and Connor lets down a ladder.

"That's pretty cool," Alec says as he climbs up first.

We all make our way up into the small room. There isn't much to it, but from the old aluminum chairs and empty ammo containers, I can tell that it had to have been just right for a hunter. Plus, the vantage point to the creek made it perfect for spotting deer.

"Where's Michael?" Claire asks.

I look down and answer, "I lost him before I found Tony."

Nobody asks any more questions about Michael. We all realize that chances are we won't run into him tonight at least. This is a huge forest and he doesn't have any gifts or abilities that could help him track us down. All we can do is pray for his safety.

Tony tells everyone about the house exploding as Carrie and my dad start passing out food. Carrie had dumped as much of the pantry as she could into a duffle bag. We all huddle together in the small, cold room under a few blankets as we pass around crackers, peanut butter, and a can of beans. A totally random combination, but we are so hungry, we could care less.

"I was looking through the binoculars at one of Blake's men when the house exploded," I say out of nowhere. I'd been going over the last few hours in my mind. "I saw a man in a ghillie suit staking out the house. A family of raccoons had come across him, not realizing that he was there. I think that one of them triggered a remote or something because one of the baby raccoons fell on something and then the man started running. I thought at first that he must have been scared of the mom, but I think he knew the explosion was inevitable."

"So they rigged the house. I wonder why," Carrie says.

"There could be several reasons. They could have been trying to kill us off. Which I would think they wouldn't do if they wanted to get their hands on Willow. Maybe Hastings had something in his house incriminating Blake…Sorry, man," Tony says to Alec when he realizes what he said.

Alec shakes his head angrily. "It's not your fault that my father is a horrible excuse for a human being."

Marya puts her arm around Alec.

"He's still your father though," I say reassuringly.

"Yes. Because of that fact, I will take him down," Alec says, his navy eyes smoldering with fury.

A few seconds later, they lighten and he relaxes his tense posture. I notice Lillie's hand on his leg and I give her a wink. She blushes and puts her hand back in her lap.

TEN

After dinner, Carrie tells the kids a story filled with magical dragons and a princess needing to be saved by her prince.

Both Sabby and Lillie are completely enamored even though their sleepy eyes are trying to droop on them. They are snuggled together under a blanket. The tree house does little to block the cold.

"We should go look for the lights. Do a little reconnaissance," Tony whispers.

We are all sitting in the furthest corner of the tree house, trying to keep things down for the kid's sake.

"I agree," I answer.

"Let me guess. You all want to go check it out while Carrie and I stay up here with the kids, huh?" my dad asks with an arched eyebrow.

I give him my puppy dog, pleading eyes.

"You know, that look isn't *always* going to work on me." He smiles. "You all just stay safe and don't stay out too long."

"We won't, Mr. Mosby," Marya says.

My dad gives her a warm smile and pats her head before he gets up to move back by Carrie and the kids.

The six of us climb down from the tree house. Connor and Alec both flip on their flashlights. The night is dark with only a sliver of the moon visible above. The air is still icy but thankfully, no snow clouds loom above us.

"I think it's to the east of here." I whisper.

Tony nods and grabs ahold of my hand as we walk in that direction. Nobody is up for conversation tonight. I can tell that all of us are feeling the exhaustion weighing heavily. Rightfully so, today has been less than relaxing.

Fifteen minutes later, I hear Claire say, "Is that it?" She points ahead of her in the distance.

Sure enough, the first glimpse of twinkling lights comes into view. "Yes, I think it is," I whisper.

Claire goes invisible and grabs Connor's hand. Tony and I follow suit, helping Alec and Marya go invisible as well. We decide to err on the side of caution in case they have guards walking the perimeter.

We walk quietly forward. The lights are only about a half-mile up ahead. It's unnerving knowing how close we were to this place in that tree house. The lights come better into view as we near the camp. They go on for as far as we can see. The camp is bordered off with metal, barbed-wire fencing. As we get closer, we can make out the shapes of tents and other temporary shelters.

Tony squeezes my hand and points up ahead.

I look in the direction. Two guards in military-grade camouflage, bolstering weapons, stand at an entrance to the camp several yards ahead. We freeze in place.

"Oh crap," Connor whispers. I turn to see him

looking down at his hands and then at Claire.

"Her invisibility isn't working," I tell Tony.

He doesn't answer.

I turn to look at his eyes. Even though the lighting is not adequate out here, I can make out their hazel-green color. "Our powers aren't working," I whisper.

"We need to go back," Tony whispers. "Now."

I nod my head and we gesture for everyone to fall back.

Thankfully, we don't run into any problems on our trip back. Our powers come back as we distance ourselves from the encampment. Nobody talks until we're safely back at the tree house. My dad lets down the ladder and we climb up.

"It's the military," Tony tells my dad assuredly.

I don't know whether that thought comforts me or freaks me out. I know that I'm partially relieved that it isn't a huge group of Blake's men. Even still, those soldiers took our friends. They took Connor's parents. They were looking for W.M. They were making sure our powers were deemed useless. What do they want with us? With me?

My dad nods his head at Tony. "Well, I don't think we have a choice on what we need to do, son."

Tony's back straightens when my dad calls him son. I can almost see a light emanating from him. That small endearment lifted him up. "I know," Tony answers, nodding his head to agree with my dad.

"I don't." Connor furrows his eyebrows in confusion. "What do we need to do?"

"We need to help get the others out," Claire says.

"I was thinking more along the lines of confronting the soldiers head on," my dad says.

"What?" I exclaim in shock. That's not at all what I thought he meant. "They would surely take us in!"

My dad shakes his head. "Willow, that could be a possibility. I served in our Army a long while ago. I believe in our country and I believe that they have our best interest in mind. No, I don't know what they are doing with our people, but I have to hold onto the hope that our people are safe under their watch. If we confront them, they should be open and honest with us about their intentions."

"That's crazy, dad! They *took* our friends! They have a device that turns off our powers! For goodness sakes, Project ELE is a complete flop! They *aren't* on our side— they can't be," I say, having no idea where in the world my dad's logic is coming from in this area.

Tony grabs my hand and laces his fingers through mine. He takes a deep breath and looks at me.

I shake my head. "Not you too!"

He smiles. *"You're beautiful when you're flustered, you know,"* he tells me in our own special way.

I blush. The comment alone brings my anxiety level down a notch.

"Look, I don't think we should all go," my dad says. "I was more so thinking along the lines of me just going in."

"No way," I say, my anxiety rising back up.

My dad straightens up and gives me a stern look. "I'm your father and you will not tell me what to do. I think

Ending ELE

this is the best course of action. I agree with you that we can't fully trust them. At least if it's just one of us, we can try and get some answers without sacrificing everyone."

"I agree with your dad." Alec cringes when I set my fiery eyes on him. "Look, it's the best course of action. If the military were going to be a danger to our people, they wouldn't have been able to get everyone out of the safe houses without killing a few. We need to find out what they want. If your dad used to be in the Army, maybe that will hold some sway with the soldiers."

"I don't like this idea at all." I cross my arms over my chest, determined now more than ever to act like a stubborn mule.

My dad gets up and moves to my side. He pulls me into his arms. "And I haven't liked the numerous times you've been put in danger. I need to do something. I need to take care of my kids and this is the only way I know how."

"I know, Dad." I sniffle into his chest. A feeling of despair is deep in the pit of my stomach. I can't lose my dad. I don't think I'd survive losing another parent.

"He'll be fine," Tony tells me.

"I hope so," I say, relenting. I realize that this argument is already lost.

After breakfast, my dad begins getting ready to head out. He gives Sabby a hug and then comes to give me one.

"I still hate this idea," I tell him stubbornly.

"Duly noted," he tells me. He says his goodbyes to

everyone else and then climbs down the ladder.

Tony has physically has to hold me back, because they've decided that we should stay here in the tree house. It would be safer because the military would certainly be out searching the perimeter the second they see my dad approach. I dig my fingernails into my palms, feeling helpless. We agreed to give him until late afternoon to return. After that, we have full rein to go after him.

We try to pass time playing I Spy and Categories with the kids. Thankfully, Connor stashed a pack of cards in his backpack. It's nearly impossible to keep my mind off my dad though, regardless of the distractions. I practice my telekinesis while we wait by folding the blanket up with my mind. Surprisingly, it works. It's not a tight or neat fold, but I manage to wad up the blanket into a messy square.

Tony massages my shoulders. "He'll be okay," he whispers.

I shiver at his breath in my ear. I can't take much pleasure in it though because I'm still so wracked with worry. I wish I could have a vision that could justify being calm.

When the sun has risen to its highest point in the sky, the sick feeling in the pit of my stomach intensifies. I stand up and declare, "We need to go now and look for him."

"If you go, we all go," Carrie interjects.

I look over at her and then down to Sabby and Lillie. I don't like that idea any more than I liked the idea of my dad going alone.

"We need to stick together," Claire says assuredly.

"Fine, we all go," I say tightly.

"Yes!" Sabby declares with an arm in the air. He has no idea how dangerous this adventure could become.

"We'll take care of them," Tony tells me.

I just nod my head. I can't find my voice; the nausea has become so intense that I can't focus right.

We pack our stuff and leave the safety of the tree house. I explain to the kids the dire need for them to stay quiet. Carrie tells them that we are on a secret mission and they beam with excitement as we set out. Sebastian makes his thumb and pointer finger turn into a gun and holds it in front of him as he walks.

Tony takes the lead and I hold onto his arm the entire way. I try to soak in some of his strength. The fear of the unknown is the worst. Not knowing if my dad is safe or what the military wants with us is unbearable. Or even the fact that if anything goes wrong, we could all be in a lot of trouble.

When we get near, we turn invisible. As we move forward, we stop every few feet to check each other's eyes. We want to get as close as we can without losing our abilities.

We stop a few yards away from the place we were last night. I turn and see the color fading from Tony's eyes. Crud.

I motion for him to step back. We step back a few feet and his eyes turn purple again. *"We need to find a better vantage point without getting any closer,"* I tell him.

"We can stay at this distance but circle the perimeter,"

he tells me. I nod my head and follow him as he leads us all through the trees.

I look down at Sabby—who is holding onto my other hand—and smile. He can't see me since we are invisible. He keeps checking his arm, his eyes wide with excitement. I guess being invisible never gets old when you're five.

We walk around the perimeter of the area, staying hidden within the trees. A few yards to the east, we find a spot with a clear view of the barbed-wire fence.

"*That's it,*" I tell Tony.

"*Yes, it is. Look, there's some people, over there by the tent.*" He points.

I squint my eyes and can barely make out their shapes. Tony's eyesight is amazing. He pulls a pair of binoculars from his bag and lifts them to his eyes.

"That snake," Tony whispers out loud. He drops the binoculars to his side, clenches his hand into a fist, and turns to look at me. His eyes are dark and angry.

"*What?*" I ask.

He hands me the binoculars. *"Look!"*

I look through the lenses towards the encampment. The two figures come into better view. I gasp. *"Michael!"*

Click.

I drop the binoculars and stiffen at the sound. In unison, we turn our heads at the same time to see three soldiers aiming their rifles at us. The lead soldier, a tall, lanky man with sun-weathered skin, looks at me with his light blue eyes. His rifle is trained carefully at Tony as opposed to me. The other two are pointing theirs in our general direction, unable to see our invisible bodies.

"Crap," I say, raising my hands. Everyone follows my lead, including Sabby and Lillie. We all let go of our invisibility and the other two soldiers aim their rifles at Alec and Conner once they can see us. They seem to be making extra efforts not to point the rifles at the kids or women. *I guess that's something,* I think to myself.

Tony is shaking, he's so angry.

"Y'all are going to need to come with us," the man with the light blue eyes says.

"We could fight. Use our powers to rip those rifles from their hands," Tony tells me without looking in my direction.

"Yes we could, but that won't help us get my dad back or any of the others. Also, there's no guarantee that one of them won't have a twitchy finger." I'm not willing to risk Tony's safety when that gun is trained on him. Even though I feel sick to my stomach, I have to trust that my vision a few days back was truth. That my friends and family will be safe like Tony told me they were on Valentine's Day. It's a small consolation, but it's all I have to hold onto right now.

"Take it nice and easy," the lead soldier says, gesturing with his gun for us to move forward. We comply and walk towards the camp, guns trained skillfully on us. I glance at Tony and see his eyes turn a hazel green.

When we reach the perimeter fence, we turn right and follow it towards the entrance. The two soldiers stare solemnly at us as we approach. We are guided into the camp. Inside the fence are tents for as far as the eyes can see. There doesn't seem to be much activity outside of the tents, other than a few soldiers walking from here to there. We see Michael and the other soldier in front of one.

In the next second, Tony darts forward, lightning quick even without his powers, and punches Michael in the face before any of us can so much as register the action. He grabs ahold of Michael's BDUs and cocks his arm back to land another punch, but stops cold when the barrel of a gun presses into his temple.

"Move back!" the soldier that Michael was speaking to earlier demands, holding the gun at Tony's head.

Tony doesn't flinch a muscle, Michael's collar still firmly in his grasp.

"Don't make this difficult," the soldier warns.

"Tony! Let him go." I run up behind him and grab ahold of his arm. Nobody stops me or trains their guns at me. Tony releases Michael's lapel and allows me to guide him a few steps back.

I turn my angry eyes at Michael. "How dare you!" I point my finger accusingly at him. I have to force myself not to follow in Tony's footsteps and punch this man's lights out. "We trusted you!" I spit vehemently.

He wipes the blood from his mouth and looks at the red smear on his hand, then looks back at me. "It's not what it seems, Willow."

My whole body is trembling with rage. "Oh really?" I spit at him. "So you aren't really a soldier? Those are just some digs you are wearing for the heck of it?" I look him up and down, snarling my lip. "You lured us! You were trying to lure me that night, weren't you?"

"His face reddens. "Yes, but not to hurt you. You're safe here. I just needed to bring you in."

"Safe? Is that why you have guns pointed at us?" Tony interjects.

I have to hold my arm out to keep him from charging forward and popping Michael again. Even though I'd like to see the man bleed a little more.

"Yes, you are. Look around. Nobody is pointing a gun at you anymore." Michael gestures behind us.

We turn around and see the others holding their rifles at their sides. The soldier next to Michael has already lowered his gun but holds it ready in case Tony goes after Michael again.

"Dad!" Sabby yells and takes off behind me. I spin around to see him fling himself into my dad's arms.

I exhale a loud swoosh of air. "Dad!" I run to him and throw my arms around him as well. He holds us both tightly. Emotions are sloshing about within me: relief, confusion, anger, and even more confusion. "What is going on?" I ask my dad, moving away so I can look into his eyes.

"I told you to wait until late afternoon. I was just about to head back to get you all when I heard the commotion," my dad tells me.

"You were going to come get us?" I ask.

He nods his head. "Yes. There is so much to tell you. The others are all here. They are safe and sound." He smiles broadly.

"They're safe?" I say absently.

He nods his head. In the next second, I see the grumpy old man walk around the corner and into view.

"Lee!" I run to his side and throw my arms around him.

He stiffens but then puts his arms around me, accepting my hug. "Hey Willow. I'm so glad you're safe!" he says back to me.

I move back awkwardly, remembering Lee's dislike for public displays of affection. "You're glad that *I'm* safe?"

"Yes! We were worried about you. Erik and I both went on the search and rescue missions with these fine soldiers." Lee gestures towards the soldiers, who have relaxed a lot more. "Who would have thunk that this Yankee would have been the one to find you?" He walks over to Michael and slaps him on the back.

Michael winces but accepts Lee's gesture of affection. "Thanks for believing in me, Lee." He rolls his eyes.

I try to circle my mind around all this craziness. I turn to look at Tony and my friends, who are just as confused as I am. "I still don't get it. Search and rescue missions? What's going on? We saw these people hauling you away. They disabled your powers and still have our powers disabled."

Lee rubs his chin between his thumb and index finger in a considering gesture. "Yeah, that's true. Truth is, we weren't too excited about the way they hauled us out of the safe house. It wasn't until we were brought here and everything was explained to us that we finally understood.

They had to disable our powers and they still have to. We can't chance the others that are out there," he points to the woods, "getting a one up on us in here."

"I'm still not following, Lee." Tony comes up and puts his arm around my waist, pulling me close to him. We lean into each other instinctively, relief clearly seen in our actions.

My dad answers for Lee. "Blake's men. They aren't just a small group; this is a massive effort on his part. In fact, he's been turning Reapers and others with our powers, but no morality, loose in this area. There are some heavy hitters in league with Blake. There is an all-out hunt for you, Willow, with a great reward for the first one to bring you in alive. It's amazing that we've made it this far without them catching us."

My jaw drops. I knew we were being hunted by Blake and his men, but I didn't think of them as being an entire army much like this one. He's been turning Reapers out on us…"Does that mean that he's injecting more people with those shots?" I ask.

Michael answers my question. "Our sources say that he still has all the people that Dr. Hastings gained control over. He's used compulsion on some of them, but a good deal of them didn't need compulsion. They're in it for the money."

I think about the masses of people that Dr. Hastings had working for him. I didn't even think about where they went or what happened to them. The things you don't clue in on when you are running for your life every other second…

"We need to take him down." Alec comes forward. "I need to be a part of taking my father down."

An older soldier, the one who had kept Tony from pummeling Michael again, nods his head. "Yes, we need to take him down. After you've all been debriefed, we can discuss our plans. If you wish to be a part of the mission, we can make it happen. You will have to be sworn in. Are you prepared for that?"

"Sworn in? Like join the military?" I ask.

He nods his head. "Yes ma'am." Sebastian jumps up and down in excitement next to me. I wonder if they'll swear in the little guy too, just for kicks.

I turn to look at Lee. "Does that mean that Erik and you were sworn in? Is that how you joined the rescue mission?"

"Along with many others, including your little friend Candy," he says.

"Candy?" I was surprised that Lee, the man that seemed to despise our government, was now one of their employees, but the news about Candy—that, I wasn't expecting.

"Yes. She's a spitfire too, a determined young woman at that," Lee says.

"Wow," is all I can say.

"I think we need to get this group to debriefing," the soldier that Michael was originally talking to announces. He turns to Tony and holds out his hand. "I apologize for pointing my gun at you, son. I'm Major Jon Heart. You can call me Jon."

Tony accepts his handshake. Jon introduces himself to all the others and of course, when it's Connor's turn for introduction, he gets a good old dose of Connor's humor.

"Major Heart, would your friends say you are a lover not a fighter?" Connor asks with a wry smile.

Jon takes it in stride and smiles. "I'm going to guess that you are Frank's boy."

Connor straightens up. "Yes sir. That's my dad."

"The humor gene must have gotten passed down to you," Jon jokes.

Connor nods proudly. "Can we see our parents now?"

Lillie jumps excitedly at Connor's side.

"Yes. We'll stop by their tent on the way to the debriefing. You will need to make it quick for now, but your little sister can stay with them. Maybe the boy too." Jon looks over at Sabby.

"I a big boy. I can be De-Bieefed." He stands tall with a hand to his forehead in a salute. I nearly lose it laughing, but hold it together for Sebastian's sake.

Jon crouches down to Sabby's level. "I know, son. I need you to take care of the girl though," he whispers so Lillie can't hear. "You know, like a real man." Sebastian's eyes glow.

"I can do that," Sabby whispers back and finishes his salute.

Jon ruffles his curls like we always do. It's that interaction that sets me at ease with Major Jon Heart. I get the distinct feeling that he must have a family too. Whether they survived the virus, I don't know. I hope for his sake they did.

Jon and Michael lead the way down a row of tents and stop at one that has its flap halfway open. "Frank?" he calls in.

Lillie and Connor don't wait for their parents to come out. They go barreling into the tent and cries of delight ring out inside.

His mom is sniffling with tears of joy when they all emerge a few minutes later. She pulls Claire into her arms and Claire gives me a huge smile over her shoulder. "I'm so happy you all are safe!" his mom says. "You have no idea the fear we had when we got here and couldn't find Lillie." She turns to us. "Thank you for keeping my daughter safe." She pulls Carrie into a hug next and then takes turns hugging and thanking the rest of us.

Jon clears his throat. "I hate to break up this beautiful reunion, but we really must get these fine people debriefed. Can you keep the kids?" he asks Connor's mom.

She nods. "Happily!" She grabs Lillie and Sabby's hand and guides them into the tent. "Guess what we have," I hear her say from inside.

"Tablets!" Sabby yells and Lillie shrieks.

I look over at Jon, who answers my question. "We have a wireless connection device and electricity."

Of course they would. They are the military after all. I wait a moment for Sebastian to turn around and protest me leaving, but he seems just fine staying here.

"We'll be back in a few," I say to Sebastian, even if only for my benefit.

We follow Jon and Michael down a few more twists and turns, deeper into the base. We end at a large tent that reminds me a lot of the medical testing station they set up outside of the mountain. The large, white tent has clear plastic windows dotted along it for yards. Inside are hallways that lead this way and that to different offices.

We are taken into what looks like a command post. A large conference table sits in the middle of the room. Three thin screens are on portable stands with projected maps and live-video feeds at one end of the room. A row of laptops and other technical equipment are on the other end.

Jon and Michael take a seat at one end of the conference table and the rest of us sit around it. Jon opens his mouth to begin speaking but then looks towards the doorway behind where I sit. I turn to follow his gaze. "Erik! Morgan!" I yell in excitement. I hop out of my seat and run to give them a hug.

"It's good to see that you made it out safe, kiddo," Erik says. His light blue eyes make a strong contrast to his black hair. It's shockingly cool. I had only seen Erik's deep black eyes.

"I see you found your man too." Morgan pats the top of my head with a smile. He lowers the blacked-out sunglasses that have always been a staple and looks at Tony. Instead of seeing the freakish white irises, he has eyes that match Erik's. Beautiful eyes. It's then that I realize he can see again. That because of the device that eliminates our powers, he's been given the gift of sight.

"Yes, I did." I smile and gesture for Tony to come meet them.

"Tony, this is Morgan. You've met Erik before. Morgan is Erik's brother," I introduce them.

Tony shakes Morgan's hand. "Nice to meet you, Morgan. Good to see you again, Erik." Tony gives him one of those side hug things that men give.

Lee interrupts our reunion. "I think we all better take a seat."

We follow suit and turn towards Jon, who has a remote in his hand that's connected to the screens behind him. He turns his head slightly to see them and clicks the remote. Three different live-video feeds pop up on the screens. My eyes open wide with interest at the images.

Jon begins the debriefing. "First, let me start off by saying that the project to remove the shields that have acted as our ozone layer failed. It took us a few weeks to realize that the ozone layer, for the most part, had in fact healed itself. There were still a few holes here and there, but it wasn't as bad as it was when we implemented the first Project ELE and put the shields up in the first place. This is why the earth didn't heat up to the temperatures we anticipated. Unfortunately, this means that we can't guarantee that the virus is gone for good. We *can* say that the epidemic has slowed quite a bit."

That's some good news, I guess. I look over at Alec and wonder if the healing ability that we have, and all the others with navy eyes have, could save people infected with the virus. I don't get to ponder on it for long because Jon goes on with the meeting.

Jon holds a laser pointer at the screen, pointing to the various images. "As you can see, these are a few of the shelters around the country."

We watch the feed where life is going on normally inside the shelters. Citizens in scrubs walk to and from places within the shelter just like normal.

Jon continues. "We need to inform you that the shelter that you were placed in was not run in the way that Dr. Hastings had been instructed to run it."

"Tell me about it," Connor interjects.

Jon frowns and grows serious. "What Dr. Hastings did was treason. He acted in the complete opposite of our instruction and performed non-sanctioned testing on the people in your shelter." He looks over at me. "Michael informs me that you found evidence that Dr. Hastings was not acting in accordance to our laws and did not have our permission to perform this testing."

"Yes sir." I nod my head.

"Good. Most people have gone into total shock when we relayed this information. Being appalled and hurt is a very common reaction." Jon says.

Claire interjects. "We were all of those things. Being made a lab rat can make you feel quite inferior. We've just had time to deal with it."

"We knew before even leaving the shelter that Dr. Hastings was scum," Alec says.

"Yes, that he was," Jon says dismissively. "I'll continue then. So you're all aware that Dr. Hastings injected the shelter's occupants with his own *untested* and *unapproved* immunizations. He also gave injections to those that he turned away from the shelter. We believe that he chose the people who he thought would work best with each gift. The people he turned away were his first round of test subjects. He studied them from inside the shelter. We found video surveillance documenting this research."

"If you found this, then why didn't you stop Dr. Hastings earlier?" Marya asks.

"We found the surveillance after the fact. We didn't realize anything was amiss at first. To be completely honest, we had not been aware that the shelter had been evacuated. Dr. Hastings must have hacked into our surveillance feed and looped past videos to make it look like everyone was still in the shelter. He continued to communicate and report to us up until his death. That was the first sign that things were off, when he stopped communicating."

I shiver, the memory of putting a bullet into Dr. Hastings sending a nasty feeling swishing through me. Tony puts his arm around me to pull me close.

"We also received a distress call from this fine soldier." Jon points to Lee.

I recall Lee's plans to try to get an S.O.S. out from Dr. Hasting's base. I hadn't even gotten a chance to find out if he had succeeded.

"We aren't proud of the fact that he pulled the wool over our eyes, but we accept responsibility for not adequately protecting the people of your shelter. We are working to make things right now. After finding Dr. Hasting's base of operations, we found evidence that a movement was being made to sell his immunizations on the black market. We also found out that several heavy hitters like Blake were searching for you, Willow. We knew we had to protect you and the others. Our first priority was to bring you and all the other survivors to safety. Then we could focus on taking down Blake and the others. They, unfortunately, are laying really low," Jon says.

"How did Michael find us?" I ask, looking at Michael, who had remained very quiet this whole time.

He holds an ice pack to his mouth and removes it to answer me. "Sheer luck. We had been tracking you all for a few days but you always stayed one step ahead of us. We figured that your powers were keeping us from finding you. I decided to go rogue. I had met Morgan and knew what he could do. I also knew that because of my memory lapses, I was hard to read. I figured that I'd have a better chance finding you on my own with that fact in my favor."

"Not to mention that you have all that freaking magnetism," Erik interjects.

My eyes widen as I look from Erik to Michael. "Magnetism? Like…you're magnetic?"

His cheeks redden as he answers me. "I wish I were magnetic. No, instead, I have the gift of magnetism, like charisma, charm." He looks away.

Erik speaks up for him. "Except times that by ten. People are drawn to him. Most people will do anything for him, just because he's freaking prince charming. His power works way better on the opposite sex." Erik seems almost jealous.

"Dude, that totally makes sense!" Alec says with recollection in his eyes.

"Wow," I say evenly. I find it unusual that Dr. Hastings would have bothered with such a gift, but I'm sure there are many ways that it can be useful. "It's kind of like compulsion then?"

Michael's expression turns to indignation. "Absolutely not. I don't force people to do things. People still have their own free will. They just kind of…find themselves next to me without even thinking about it."

"Oh, okay. Noted." I look away from his intense expression. I can tell he struggles with how he feels about his own gift. "Sorry."

"It's okay." Michael shrugs his shoulders and clears his throat. "Anyway, I wasn't lying about waking up in a hospital by myself. I don't know at what point I was injected with one of Dr. Hastings magical shots. I didn't even realize I had a gift until after I turned to the military for help. I had been working with a recruiter and planned to be sworn into the Army. The train wreck happened before I was able to do that. Naturally, I turned to them for help when I woke up in an abandoned hospital. The first time I looked in the mirror, I thought that they had given me an eye transplant when I was in the coma. It was the creepiest thing ever. Then I went searching through the hospital, only to find it deserted. I thought I was in a nightmare—that none of it could be real. I didn't know what to do. After spending a few days there by myself, I managed to transmit a message to 9-1-1 through a tablet with a battery on its last legs. Jon and his team came and got me that night."

"He was one of the first people with powers that we found, even though it took us a while to figure out what power he had. We found him after finding Dr. Hastings's base," Jon includes.

Michael says proudly, "And I got sworn in that evening."

"And that circles us back around to how you found us," Tony says.

Michael's brown eyes look down shyly. "I'm sorry I lied to you all. I didn't know what to do. I had been told that you wouldn't be trusting, so I immediately went in with a story planned out. Some of it was the truth and as you now know, some of it I made up."

"He had your best interests in mind," Lee says, taking up for Michael.

Michael looks at Tony and me with hopeful eyes.

"I understand, man. I'm sorry I hit you," Tony says.

"I guess I kind of deserved it." Michael smiles but then winces and raises the ice pack back up to his lip.

"We forgive you," I announce for everyone. I look around, hoping I didn't speak out of turn, but they all nod their heads in agreement.

"So, what does Blake want with Willow?" Connor asks.

I roll my eyes and answer for Jon. "My blood. Exactly what he's wanted all along."

"Yes, he has some high bidders who are willing to pay almost anything for your powers. They have already sold Dr. Hastings's formulas to some weapons dealers in the Middle East. Thankfully, there isn't a formula for your powers, Willow." Jon looks over at Tony. "Or is there?"

"No, there isn't. This is just a fluke," Tony says sternly.

I give Jon a look that tells him not to question us further.

He nods his head in understanding. "Understood." I can tell though, that this won't be the last time we're questioned about this.

"So what's the plan now?" Alec asks, eager to find his father and bring him in.

"Now that we have you here, safe, we hunt for Blake and his men," Jon says.

"I want in on that," Alec says.

"We can make that happen."

"Me too," Tony and I say in unison. We turn and smile at each other. Marya, Claire, and Connor agree.

My dad says, "I've already been sworn in." He smiles.

"All right then. We will have a ceremony later this evening. For now, let's get everyone situated and fed," Jon says.

We all agree and head out to find our new homes and the cafeteria hall.

Ending ELE

Prior to dinner, we are sworn in—in front of a large crowd of three hundred plus soldiers. Afterwards, dinner turns into one big family reunion. We move from table to table, catching up with everyone that we knew from the safe houses and the shelter. Lee convinces Jon to allow us to host a bonfire like we used to do to celebrate at the first safe house. We even scrounge up the makings for s'mores.

Over the campfire and impromptu musical performances, Claire, Marya, and I catch up with Candy. Turns out that she and Jake are doing great. She lets us know that she's officially in love. We ooh and ahh while talking about our men. Candy has loved being a part of the military so far. She finds it exciting and fulfilling.

I break away after we catch up and go in search of Audrey, Morgan's wife. I find Molly along the way. She breaks away from her public make-out session with Seth. Thankfully, she doesn't instigate too much of a conversation with me. She says hello and goes back to lip locking with Erik and Morgan's younger brother. I shake my head, remembering how difficult she was to get along with back at the first safe house.

"Willow!" Audrey calls from a few feet away. She meets me in the middle and gives me a heartwarming hug.

"It's so good to see you, Audrey!" I say, looking up at her. She's still exotically beautiful. Her eyes are the color of gold, not too far off from the copper pot that they were when she was in full power.

We talk and catch up until Tony interrupts. "Mind

if I take Willow out for a spin?" he asks Audrey.

She grins slyly. "Why, of course not." She grabs my hand and pulls me closer to her so she can whisper in my ear before I go. "I will be your bridesmaid." She laughs at my shocked expression. "I saw it," is all she says before turning and walking in Morgan's direction.

My heart thumps in my chest and my face flushes red. I can't help the Cheshire grin that spreads across my face.

Tony pulls me into his arms and begins swaying side to side. "What did she say?" He gives me a funny look.

For once, the lack of powers comes in handy here. We are just two normal teens in a relationship, not reading each other's minds. Two teens that are soon to be married? My stomach does a funny flutter. "Oh nothing," I answer, pressing my cheek into his chest as we sway to the music.

"We're finally safe," Tony whispers in my ear.

"Yes, I suppose we are," I say quietly. Although, we won't be completely safe until Blake is stopped. I decide not to bring that up. Why ruin this moment?

"I love you, Willow." Tony runs his fingers through my hair and pulls my hair back lightly so I'm looking up at him.

I giggle at the gesture but stop when I see the smoldering look in his eyes. "I love you too, Tony."

He kisses me. Slow and sweet at first and then heavy and passionately. The mammoth moths in my stomach flutter heavily. I lean my forehead against his, hoping no one saw that.

Ending ELE

"Where do we go from here?" Tony asks, his voice husky and out of breath.

"We kick bad guy butt!" Connor jumps out from nowhere. That or he had been standing there the whole time and we were too busy to pay attention.

"They were having a moment." Claire slaps his arm. He rebuttals by pulling her into his arms, dipping her, and giving her a hot kiss. He sets her back on her feet a moment later. She leans into him, trying to overcome the dizziness. Her cheeks are flushed.

I can't help but laugh. They are adorable.

We spend the rest of the party hanging out and trying not to talk about the elephant in the room. For tonight, we are only teenagers with not a care in the world.

ELEVEN

It's amazing how fast time passes when you're having fun.

Being in the company of all of my family and friends and knowing that they are safe and healthy is amazing. The past six weeks have passed by in a blur.

Training exercises, military classes, and field missions keep our days busy. At night, we spend time around the new military tradition—the bonfire. It's a good way to socialize and stay warm. The snow still continues but is starting to be scarcer as we move into the second week of February.

We've had a few hot leads on Blake's whereabouts. Unfortunately, he remains a step ahead of us each time we investigate the lead. Alec is trying to keep his frustration from showing but I know it's not easy on him. I can tell he just wants to put this behind him and move on.

I look over at him walking towards the operation tent with Marya. I squeeze Tony's hand and give him a warm smile. The two of us have grown closer than even before. We've spent every night getting to know more about one another. We talk about our favorite movies and memories from our childhood. We even talk about my mom and his parents, about how their deaths have affected us. When we run out of things to say, we just sway to the music until our eyelids are too heavy to stay open. I share a bunk tent with Marya, Claire, and Candy. When I'm not sleeping, I'm with Tony though.

  We walk into the operations tent and take a seat in one of the fold-out chairs in their meeting room. At least fifty other soldiers join us today. We've been having these regular meetings to plan and strategize.

  I try to fight off the nervous jitters I experience when Jon takes the stage. I know how this meeting will go. We will go over our attempts thus far, any known leads on Blake's location, and then he will ask for any suggestions. I haven't told Tony, but today I plan to speak up—it's time.

  Jon begins the meeting and we all sit quietly to take everything in. Like it's been for the past week, we have no new leads. "I'm going to go ahead and open the floor for suggestions now."

  I timidly raise my hand. Tony looks over at me with surprise.

  "Willow." Jon points to me.

  I slowly stand up from my seat. I fiddle with a loose piece of thread on my sweater sleeve, trying to avoid focusing on all the eyes that peer in my direction. I haven't discussed this idea with Tony yet and I have no idea what he will say. I think I've known for a while now what needs to be done. My vision showed me what would happen. Valentine's day is two days away. Unfortunately, I didn't see much past Tony's proposal to know if this plan will succeed or not.

"I propose..." I cringe at the use of the word propose. I clear my throat and start again. "I *suggest* that Tony and I set a trap for Blake and his men. They need to think that we are somewhere within their reach. We can lay the bait and hope they take it. They haven't shown their faces in a while, but I doubt they can resist ignoring us if we are outside and vulnerable."

Tony stands up at my side. "Why didn't you tell me this?" he asks in a hushed whisper.

"I'm sorry; I didn't want you to stop me," I whisper back. I look forward at Jon, who is speaking with a few other higher ups in hushed tones. I assume they are contemplating my idea.

Tony whispers back, "I wouldn't have stopped you, Willow. I just would have liked to know."

My heart jerks at the sound of hurt in his voice. I turn and look into his eyes. "I'm sorry, Tony."

"You need to trust me," he says back.

"I do," I whine, my face red with embarrassment. I know there must be several eyes still on us, even though they don't outright stare. Anyone sitting close to us can still hear our whispered conversation.

Thankfully, Jon is back up at the podium and interrupts our disagreement. "Are you aware of the risks to your safety, Ms. Mosby?"

I nod my head. "Yes sir."

"We can have soldiers spread out through the area but there is no guarantee that they will be able to protect you," Jon states again.

"Yes, I understand." I look over at Tony, who is gritting his teeth.

"Where do you suppose we should lay this trap?" Jon asks.

"My cabin," Tony says. His body is rigid with tension as he looks forward at Jon.

"Blake has already looked for you there once," Jon counters.

"Yes, but he wouldn't blame us for going back again," Tony says.

"The area is a good one with a lot of coverage for us to put men out there," Michael interjects.

Jon seems to mull this over for a few moments, and then says, "Okay. We'll try this. At the first sign of danger, we are pulling you two out though."

"Understood," I say quickly.

Tony only nods his head and says, "Yes sir." His hands are balled up into fists—the number one sign that he's not happy about this.

Jon dismisses the meeting but calls for Tony and me to meet in the conference room in thirty minutes.

I walk out of the tent and into the cold February air. Tony walks passed me and glances over his shoulder, giving me a non-verbal command to follow him.

We walk down a row of tents to an area just behind the cafeteria. He stops and spins around on me. "What do you think you were doing back there?" he asks. His eyes are intensity personified.

"I had a vision. A while back. We were in your cabin on Valentine's Day," I tell him.

He looks surprised. Normally, we tend to have similar visions, but I can tell by his expression that this is news to him. "Okay, but that doesn't explain why you would offer yourself up as bait without discussing it with me. That is what the old Willow would do. I thought you grew out of that impulsive behavior."

Ouch. His comment stings a bit, because it's true. "Yeah, well, the old Willow would have impulsively offered herself up as bait alone. The new Willow offered up her boyfriend and herself as bait this time."

Something softens in Tony's hard gaze. A muscle twitches at the corner of his mouth.

I take the opportunity and close in on it, moving forward to wrap my arms around his middle. I look up at him, my face only inches from him. "You know you want to laugh," I whisper.

His face softens some more. "I really just want to protect you, Willow. I want to shield you from all this. I want to do away with the bad guys and get on with our life."

"I know. We aren't getting any closer to finding Blake though. I had to have had that vision for a reason, Tony." *And not just to predict my proposal*, I think. "This could be why. We could finally end this."

"I am glad you are thinking in the *we* sense now. I just can't help but worry," Tony says. "Did you see us catch Blake? Were we safe?" Tony asks.

This is a moment where the easiest thing would be to

lie. I could tell him—*sure, we made it out just fine.* Then he could go into this mission feeling confident. That wouldn't be a way to begin an engagement though. I mentally kick myself for continuing to fret over the proposal. *Business Willow, business.* I tell myself to focus. I need to be truthful with the man I love. "I didn't see what happened after we were in your cabin. I woke up. Up until then, we were safe. I can't tell you that I know how this will end, because I don't."

Tony chews on my words for a few seconds, his gaze lost in thought. "Okay, fair enough." He kisses the bridge of my nose. "If we're going to be the bait, then we better get ourselves prepared."

He takes my hand and together, now unified, we walk back to the conference room.

Jon, Michael, and a few other higher ups, go over our plans with us. We decide that the best thing would be to head out to Tony's cabin tomorrow night. This gives us the rest of today and the first part of tomorrow to prepare. Tony's cabin is a three-hour walk from here. With our powers, we could get there in thirty minutes. However, that would mean that we wouldn't have adequate protection since many of the soldiers don't have super powers.

When we conclude the meeting and head out of the tent, the sun has already descended behind the mountains. We go straight to the cafeteria, where we are barraged with dozens of questions and concerns from our family and friends. In the end, we field all the questions and go off to bed, in hopes of getting a decent night's sleep before our mission.

TWELVE

"Are you sure you want to do this?" my dad asks me when I'm preparing my stuff to go out.

He hasn't questioned my idea or decision yet, so it was only a matter of time.

"Yes, Dad. I need to do this," I tell him.

"I know," he sighs. "You are just like your mom in that way. Determined and not willing to allow anything to stand in her way." He runs his hand over my curls. This time, his fingers don't get stuck. He seems disappointed by that. Like that's our thing.

"I love you, Dad," I tell him.

"Love you too, baby." He gives me a hug.

Sabby joins us, crushing our legs with his normal five-year-old strength. "I wuv you, Wello."

I lean down and kiss the top of his head. "You too, bud."

Tony clears his throat when he comes up to the doorway of my dad's tent. "Are you ready, Willow?"

I swallow my nervous anxiety. "Yes, ready as I'll ever be."

"Okay, the others are by the cafeteria hall. They

want to wish you luck." Tony tells me.

They are going to be part of the group that will be hiding around the perimeter of the cabin. I feel kind of bad that they will be sleeping outside while we are out of the elements.

"Bye Dad, bye Sabby." I wave at them as I walk out of the tent. Tony doesn't move to follow me. "Are you coming?" I ask.

"I wanted to speak to your dad really quick if you don't mind," Tony says. "I'll catch up to you in a few."

I nod and head towards the cafeteria. I laugh when I turn the corner and see Claire and Marya in camo gear with their faces painted to match. Alec and Connor turn the corner dressed in similar outfits. Connor's face paint looks horrendous. I double over laughing.

"He wouldn't let me do his makeup!" Claire laughs along with me.

"You should have let her," Alec says, laughing as well.

It takes a few minutes for us to stop laughing at Connor, who literally painted his face to look like a clown with rings around his eyes and a smile around his lips in dark green. It takes a lot for us to stop laughing at him. I have to hold onto my side because it hurts from the exertion.

"You should let me redo it." Claire giggles as she says it. "You aren't supposed to make it look like face makeup. You just smudge the colors together here and there to blend in with your environment."

Now Connor is huffing with his hands over his chest. "Fine."

Claire blows him a kiss and takes his hand to lead him back to the bathroom. Tony rounds the corner before they make their escape and he falls to the floor laughing.

"Not cool man, not cool!" Connor stomps away towards the bathroom.

This sends us all back into our laughing fit. Claire's face is red with the effort of trying to control herself when she moves to follow Connor.

"This looks like a disciplined group of soldiers," Jon calls out from behind us.

We all straighten up and turn to face him at attention like we've been trained. Hey, you can't blame us—we're still minors.

"At ease," he says, smiling. "Are you ready?"

"Yes sir," Tony and I say at the same time.

"Good. You should probably head out now. The sun is beginning to set, so you should have decent enough cover. We'll be following close behind you. You won't see us though. Try to pretend like we don't exist," Jon reminds us.

"Will do, sir," Tony says.

I check the weapon on my hip and the other one at my ankle. Tony does the same. We grab our duffels and make our way out of the safety of the camp.

The moon is full tonight, making it easy to travel without a flashlight. I want desperately to be able to hightail it to Tony's cabin, but I have to force myself to maintain a normal speed. Our powers came back to us before we even left the camp.

In accordance with our plan, they turned off the disabling device and Jon is carrying it with him as we speak. This meant that they had to leave most everyone with light blue eyes, including Candy, back at the base to protect the others. It was a necessary decision because that device could be the difference between us being able to stop Blake or not. Jon will enable the device at the first opportune time when Blake is in range. It's pretty clever. However, this will put us all on even playing field in a fight. I prefer to keep my powers, but I understand that this is the better option for the majority.

Tony stops and grabs my hand to stop me. *"Did you feel that?"*

I try to open up my senses even though my heart is pounding fast. *"What is...?"* My thoughts are cut off as I'm barraged by an overwhelming sensation of slimy evil. *"Is it Blake?"* It can't be. I know we are safe in Tony's cabin on Valentine's Day.

"I don't think so." Tony throws me to the ground in the next second. He crashes onto me just as a bullet swishes past us and into the trunk of a tree.

"Stay down," Tony demands as he uses his body as a shield over mine. We both go invisible. I try to move my head to look around for our assailant, but I can't move but a few inches with Tony on top of me.

Two more bullets sink into a tree to the right of us.

"He can't see us," I tell Tony. Thank goodness.

"I'll sneak up on him. You take cover," Tony says as he starts to move off me.

"But..." I say, but Tony cuts me off.

"Take cover," he says again sternly.

Even though I don't want to obey, I do. Tony army crawls towards the direction that the shots came from.

I army crawl in the opposite direction, towards a fallen tree. It's amazing how easy an army crawl is when I have the power of strength. Back in training, when our powers were turned off, this effort alone would have me panting. I quickly make my way around the tree. When I'm safely behind it, I sneak a peek in the direction that Tony went. I try to focus my vision better to see him through the dense foliage.

I finally spot the assailant not too far from where I am. He's dressed in all black, looking through the scope of his rifle. He opens his eyes and I see the light blue. He can see us! He trains his rifle on Tony.

"No!" I yell as I hop out from behind the tree and start running in his direction. The rifle swings towards me and, as if in slow motion, I see his finger pull back on the trigger a second before Tony clobbers him in the head from behind.

I am knocked back by the force of the bullet, which hits me in the chest a millisecond later.

"Willow!" Tony cries out. The sound of his voice seems so far away as my head hits the ground and my world goes dark.

THIRTEEN

The sound of a log losing its hearty fight against the raging fire startles me awake.

My heart is racing. I refuse to open my eyes, worried that I'll see the stark fluorescent lights and grey concrete walls of a place I vaguely remember. A terror strong enough to taste fills my senses. I remember the dream that woke me. I was back in the room that Zack held me in. Blake was towering over me with a snarl on his face. I try to tell myself that I'm not there. *I'm not there*. It's been months since I've had that dream.

The panic dissipates when I force myself to open my eyes and I see the wooden rafters of Tony's cabin. I blink my eyes a few times, trying to force the exhausted haziness from my vision. I look over at the piece of wood that has fallen through the grate in the fireplace. It morphs into brilliant, orange-red glowing embers. My heart rate steadies out as I watch the embers slowly progress to nothing more than grey ash.

I try to move, but my chest aches. Then I remember the bullet that slammed into my bulletproof vest. *Tony!* He took down the man that shot me, but were there any others?

I notice the steady rise and fall of Tony's breathing behind me and I sigh in relief. *He's here and I have nothing to fear…* For now.

"Don't think about it, not today," Tony says to me in our special form of mind speak, which only the two of us share.

I could fret on the fact that we are waiting for the big fish to bite into the bait but, instead, I decide to take his advice and relish in this moment. To allow myself to feel safe and secure with his warm arm draped across my middle. To memorize the way my head fits perfectly under his chin. Suddenly, I feel as though we aren't close enough. The stubble on his cheek tickles my forehead as I look up at him. His eyes are still closed and he looks endearingly innocent in his partial slumber. I stretch up and give him a small kiss on his sleeping lips. He smiles and his eyes flutter open. I can't get enough of those eyes, with the colors that mimic mine so perfectly.

They are still a deep navy blue from, I assume, when he used his healing power on me last night. I search those beautiful eyes. The prism of other colors are still visible when the light hits them just right and the ever-present red fleck sits towards the inside portion of his irises.

"Morning," he says aloud in a scratchy voice.

I can't help but feel a longing to hold him closer, to somehow become a single entity. It's been over a month since I've woken up next to Tony. Back at the base camp, we sleep in separate rooms—as it should be when one is not on the run for their lives. I'm not going to think of that…

"Morning," I say before I brush my lips against his once again. This time his lips crush into mine as he melts into our kiss.

"Happy Valentine's Day," Tony tells me.

My heart starts thudding in my chest. I've been dwelling on this day for a while now—it always seemed so far away. But, here we are.

Tony gives me a half-grin, taking in my expression and thinking that I forgot. *"You don't even remember the big day of love?"* He chuckles more so to himself, as if I amuse him in a completely adorable, loving kind of way.

I shove his chest lightly in a playful gesture. "With all that's been going on, I'm surprised you remembered."

"Actually, Sabby reminded me. He said I better get you something good." He winks at me.

"I bet he did." I smile at him. My heart is still beating quickly. I throw my shield up and Tony gives me a startled look. I ignore it and try not to think of the vision. *They don't always play out exactly the same in reality*, I remind myself. Things change and are molded by circumstances. I need to stop thinking about what's about to happen. I sit up and look at him. "Happy Valentine's Day to you, Tony. I'm sorry I didn't get you anything." This is the first time I noticed the disarray of the house. I guess that last encounter with Blake's men here didn't go unscathed.

He kisses me on the tip of my nose. "You are all I could ever want, Willow Mosby." He grins excitedly, then hops up and goes to place another log into the fire. The fire crackles and comes back to life. Sitting back down next to me, he pulls me back into his arms, kissing the top of my head. He gently caresses my back with his hand, sending goose bumps down to my toes.

I feel his body shift as he brings my face up to his. "Will you come upstairs for a second? There's something I want to give to you."

I nod my head and give him a shaky smile. My legs shake as I stand up off the couch. Oh my gosh…Oh *my* gosh…

He takes my hand in his and leads me to his parent's room. I take a deep breath as he opens the door and gestures for me to take a seat on the red chaise lounge near the bay window. My palms go sweaty and my head feels light and airy as I watch him rummage through the closet. He removes a panel in the wall to reveal a safe. He turns to grin at me in excitement before he looks back at the safe and turns the dial several times. He must not notice the nervous expression on my face. I force myself to take a few deep breaths to compose myself. *Enjoy this*, I tell myself. A moment like this only comes once in a lifetime.

A second later, I hear a click as the safe is opened. While I can't see the contents, I can hear him shift papers and items around inside it before he carefully takes out a long, black box.

"Close your eyes," he says to me with a goofy grin.

I bite my lip but oblige. My legs bounce in anticipation as I hear him moving things around inside the black box. Then it snaps shut and I can hear him placing it back in the safe, securing it. The panel on the wall snaps back and I listen to him walk over to where I'm sitting, just like in my vision. With my eyes still shut, he takes my hand in his.

"Can I open them now?" I ask impatiently. I need to see his eyes. I need to know that Tony is going to do this because he thought of it all on his own and not because he saw my vision. He doesn't answer me immediately and I get more fidgety. I can feel his palm sweating in my hand.

"Okay, you can open them now," he tells me. His voice is soft, almost a whisper.

I let out a shaky breath and squeeze my eyes one last time before I open them. Tony is kneeling in front of me with my hand still in his. His other hand holds a small box and he places it in my lap.

My mouth goes dry and I suddenly forget how to speak. I have already played this vision over and over again in my mind. Now that it's happening in real time, I can scarcely keep from passing out.

"Open it," he urges me.

I take a deep breath and decide to change the vision slightly. I take a leap of faith, hoping the box doesn't contain a pair of earrings. I pull Tony up off his knees so that he's sitting beside me. He looks at me with confusion as I hold the closed box in between my hand and his. "I have a confession to make," I say as I lean my forehead against his. My breathing is heavy and so is his.

"Oh yeah? What is it?" He pulls away slightly and

his eyes drift down to my lips.

I accentuate the next word I say. "Yes," I tell him.

His gaze darts away from my lips and back up to my eyes. It takes him a second to register. I let go of my shield and in the next second, his eyes turn black. He smiles wide as he feels the excitement and love flowing out of me. "You knew this was going to happen? You had a vision?"

I nod sheepishly.

He pulls me into his arms and crushes his lips against mine. Our hearts meld together in a ferocious beat of excitement. He pulls back, his breathing heavy. "I still want to do this the proper way."

The giddiness grows inside me as I nod excitedly at him.

"Go ahead, open it," he tells me.

I look down and slowly remove the lid to the tiny box. Inside sits the most beautiful ring I've ever seen…I mean, that I've ever seen in real life. I look deep into Tony's eyes—love is overflowing from the both of us.

Tony clears his throat. "Willow Mosby…" Just the way he says my name makes my heart get caught in my throat. "You mean everything to me; you're my whole world. My life begins and ends with you. After my parents died, I never thought I could love again, never thought I could be normal…until you came along. You turned my world upside down and taught me what it is to be a man. You showed me how to live and that love can happen, even in the darkest of times. I need you like I need air." He squeezes my hand in his. "I want to spend the rest of my life with you. Would you do me the honor of becoming my wife?"

Tears spring to my eyes as I try to find humor enough to say, "I already told you my answer."

He laughs a nervous laugh.

I look down at the ring and back up at Tony. I love this man in front of me all the way to the core of my being. I need to give him a real answer. A tear slips down my cheek as my heart soars. I purse my lips to keep from crying and nod my head. "Yes." My voice catches as I repeat my well-thought-out answer.

A huge smile spreads across his face and all the nervousness he was experiencing is now gone in an instant. He wastes no time taking the ring from the box and gliding it on my finger. As if he'd had it sized just for me, it fits perfectly. The other half of the ring lies in the box, the part I will receive when we say our vows. *I'm engaged*, I say over and over again in my mind.

"*We're engaged*," he corrects me with a proud smile. Then he adds out loud, "This ring belonged to my mom. I brought their rings back here…after they died." This time his voice catches. "I suppose you already knew that?"

I nod my head as my eyes well with tears. That fact makes the significance of this gift all the more meaningful. I hold my hand up in the light and admire the stunning ring. It's platinum, set with a beautiful, princess-cut sapphire surrounded by six intricately cut diamonds.

I am immediately lost in Tony's arms, clinging to the man I deeply love. I don't want to let him go. I don't want to return to our reality. I know what awaits us. I can sit here and grieve about our loss of innocence, or I can enjoy this memory in the making.

My hand starts shaking and Tony pulls me tightly to him. He pets my hair with his hand in a soothing gesture. "Don't think about it, Willow. Not today. Today is ours—not theirs. We won't let them take away this moment," he whispers into my ear.

"I know," I tell him. I pull back from him. "Did you ask my dad?" I remember how Tony had asked to speak to my father before we left.

He nods his head. "Yeah, what do you think took me so long to catch back up with you? I got the usual interrogation but in the end, he gladly gave me his permission."

I grab ahold of his hand and, using Morgan's gift, I'm drawn back to the moment he asked my dad.

A tear falls from my father's eye as he tells Tony, "You make my daughter happy and I know that she makes you happy. A love like yours only comes around once. While I still think of her as my baby girl, I know that circumstances have made the two of you grow up much faster than you should have. I appreciate you asking my permission first." My dad takes a deep breath before finishing. "I give you permission to marry my one and only daughter so long as she'll have you."

Tony exhales the breath he'd been holding. "Thank you, Mr. Mosby." His voice is thick with emotion.

My dad pulls him into a tight hug. "Call me Dad."

Tony's eyes water and he does his best to blink away

the tears.

I pull out of the memory and smile at Tony. "That's amazing," I tell him.

"I know," he says, before pulling me into another noteworthy kiss.

Tony and I spend the day passing time. We spent a few hours putting the house back together, turning back over upturned furniture, sweeping leaves and whatnot out of the house, and fixing the hinges on the door. All these little things made it seem more homey, but the looming dread of what was to inevitably come was always in the back of our minds.

Every chance I had to look at the ring, I did. I just couldn't get over its beauty and the fact that it was on the ring finger of my left hand. When Tony was screwing in the hinges for the door, I was staring at it. When I had my hands on the broom, I was staring at it. I'm pretty sure Tony has noticed but he hasn't said anything. I still catch him smiling like an eight-year-old at a birthday party out of the corner of my eyes.

When the house is pretty much put back together, we both collapse on the couch. Tony fed the fire a few more logs and the crackling of the fire makes me want to just sink into Tony and relax…Well, as much as one could while knowing they're being hunted.

I guess part of me feels relief knowing that there are people out there around the perimeter of the house watching over us. I still can't help feeling unsettled though.

Tony takes my left hand into his just as an ember crackles in the fire. "It really does look lovely on your hand." He runs his thumb over the sapphire.

I look up at him and give him a sheepish smile. "I know," I say goofily.

He lets out a small chuckle at my confidence. He leans down next to my ear and whispers, "I can't wait until the other part is on there too."

He means the wedding band. A pleasant shiver runs up and down my arms. "Me neither," I whisper back, lost in thought about what married life will be like. In my mind, I envision children playing in a spacious yard while Tony and I watch from rocking chairs on a wraparound porch.

"I wonder what life will be like," I say. "Like, if we will have children and live in a house with a white picket fence…" I say, lost in thought.

I feel a smile tug at Tony's lips from atop my head. "I want to have two children," he says in reply. "One boy and one girl. We'll name them Ashton and Annabeth."

I look back up at him after zoning in on my ring for the billionth time that day. "And how long have you had those names picked out?" I ask playfully. I never thought about having children…much less what their names would be if I did.

"Awhile," he says cryptically. "I want them to have your hair and smile. They'll be the most beautiful kids in the world."

I lean my head back and look back up at Tony. "I

want them to have your personality and skin."

He gives me a little laugh. "My skin?" he questions.

"Yes! I love the tone of your skin. It's the perfect color—like you've been kissed by the sun."

He rubs the side of my arm that's wrapped around him and grins, pulling me closer.

Just then, a gunshot sounds off in the distance, pulling Tony and me out of our lovesick trance. Tony pulls me down to the floor, protecting me from the what-ifs. He reaches under the sofa and pulls out two guns he had stashed there earlier while we were cleaning, handing one to me. I make sure the safety is on and stash it in my waistband. Tony rises up just enough to see out of the window without being detected.

"What do you see?" I ask impatiently. He looks out for a few moments before joining me back onto the floor.

"Nothing, that's what scares me the most." He looks at me with his hazel eyes.

"It's Blake," I say in an exhale.

"How do you know?" Then the realization hits him as he looks into my eyes. "They turned on the device," he whispers.

I let out a shaky breath. Our deal was that they would turn on the device when Blake and his men were in range. This means they are in range. I feel vulnerable as the realization dawns on me that we won't be utilizing our abilities on possibly the most important fight of our lives. The only thing that is comforting is the fact that they won't have a leg up on us either.

Another gunshot sounds off in the distance and I instinctively cringe. I hate that sound even more knowing I can't heal the instant one of us gets shot.

I bite off a scream when a smoke bomb crashes through the window and starts filling the room.

Tony grabs my hand. "We stay together," he says quickly, while squeezing my hand.

"Got it," I say in reply. I don't plan on going anywhere without Tony. I hold onto the back of his shirt as we crawl through the smoke towards the back door.

A peppering of gunshots spray through the window behind us. Tony opens the door in just enough time for us to dive out of it.

He grabs the back of my shirt and lifts me to my feet. I catch a glimpse of his neon eyes as we begin running towards the cover of the trees.

"Our powers are working. They must have turned off the machine," I tell Tony as we make ourselves invisible.

"I'm not sure if that's a good thing or a bad thing," he tells me.

We take cover behind the base of a large evergreen and watch the cabin. Men dressed in black from head to toe circle around the perimeter, firing shots into the cabin.

"Didn't I warn those idiotic guns for hire that I'd slit their throats if they damaged the package?" a familiar voice says from behind me.

My blood runs arctic cold as I place the voice and his annoying habit of turning everything into a question. I barely notice the sound of rapid gunfire and fighting behind us at the cabin. I turn to look at the hunter who thinks I'm nothing more than a lab rat. "Blake," I say through my teeth.

Tony instinctively moves his body in front of mine as a shield to protect me from the gun that Blake is pointing in my direction. "You should go ahead and surrender now, Blake." Tony spits on the ground in front of Blake's shoe.

Blake looks at it with disgust. "And why would I do that? Do I not have your house surrounded?" His eyes widen with surprise a moment later. He shines his flashlight up into Tony's eyes. "Now, now, isn't this interesting?" He clucks his tongue. "Looks like someone's been sharing her blood, hasn't she?" He looks at me like I'm nothing more than a filthy prostitute.

"I can do whatever I want, you overrated, worthless piece of crap that tries to pass himself off as a human," I retort, realizing how childlike that just sounded but happy to have him think that I gave Tony my blood. Rather that, than him wonder how Tony got his multiple gifts. I smile at him and feel a little smug when his face contorts with rage. That's why what happens next knocks me from my feet. Literally. I'm knocked off my feet when a bullet slams into my shoulder, just to the left of the bulletproof vest.

"Bastard!" Tony yells as he whips the gun from Blake's hand using his telekinesis and throws Blake against a tree. He drops to the ground beside me in the next second. His hand is on my shoulder, trying to stop the blood and heal me at the same time.

It hurts so bad. I didn't expect the excruciating fire

and pure, raw ache that your body feels when metal is pounded through your flesh and muscles at unstoppable speeds. I feel woozy and blackness is closing in on my vision. I blink it away when I see three of Blake's men running in our direction. I focus my powers, weak as they are, on one of them. I lift him up from the ground and with a flick of the wrist I throw him into another man. Both of them go flying backwards a sprawl of arms and legs as they hit the trunk of a tree.

Tony pulls both of his hands up, one red with my blood. He sends the other man flying backwards.

I look down at my shoulder. It's still gushing blood. The pain has lessened enough to keep me from passing out but it still remains unbearably intense. I try to focus my own healing abilities while Tony tries to stop Blake's oncoming attack. My brain is too foggy and my heart is beating so hard I can feel it in my ears and in my temples.

I watch as Tony lifts Blake in the air but Blake falls to the ground a millisecond later. Tony lifts his hand as if to pick Blake back up but nothing happens.

The pain is increasing in my shoulder and I cry out in pain. Our powers are turned off.

"No!" Tony yells. "Not yet! Turn the machine off!" He looks down at my tortured expression.

Over Tony's shoulder, I barely make out Blake getting up and grabbing the gun. I know I should call out and warn Tony but everything is foggy and my throat is closing up on me.

Tony turns around just in time for the two of us to

watch Blake get pummeled by his son. Alec jumps on top of him and begins punching him over and over again. I can see the snow turning dark around Blake's head…Or is that the world turning dark…

"Willow! Stay with me, Willow!" Tony calls to me from somewhere in the dark fog.

If I go to him, I will feel the pain. If I stay where I'm at, I get the sweet relief that this darkness brings me.

"Turn the freaking thing off now!" he yells at the top of his lungs. It's enough to make me want to open my eyes, but I don't. The darkness feels so good, so I let it carry me away.

EPILOGUE

"Yes," I breathe to Tony with a smile on my face. "I do."

"Then I now pronounce you man and wife. You may kiss the bride." Tony wastes no time wrapping his arms around me and kissing me with a passion unmatched by any other. I melt in his arms as the kiss prolongs more than it probably should.

He leaves me breathless when he pulls away and the crowd of guests bursts into applause. I blush as I look to my bridesmaids and then to the crowd. I catch my dad's gaze as he wipes a tear away from his eyes and I almost cry again.

Today has been a day filled with happy, bittersweet tears. Tears that my dad has to let me go. Tears that my mom can't be here today. Tears of joy that I can now call Tony my husband. Tears of relief that life is finally returning to normal. At least as normal as life will ever be.

It's hard to believe that only a month ago Blake and his men were taken down. Alec got the pleasure of arresting him just like he wanted. I didn't get to see everything since I was completely passed out. Marya tells me that it was awesome though. She was the one that ran and got Jon to turn the machine off for me. I woke up the following day in the medical wing of the camp, surrounded by all of my family and friends. After that fateful day, life was a blur of debriefings, testifying in court at Blake's trial, capturing the rogue Reapers, helping to plan the release of the other shelters, and of course, planning our wedding. No wonder it all happened in the blink of an eye.

Tony envelopes his hand in mind, bringing me back to this amazing moment. I wrap my hand in his. We smile at each other as we walk back down the aisle. Cheerful clapping along with some hoots and hollers from our friends sound out as we reach the sanctuary doors.

We walk out and into a tiny room off to the side to gain some privacy before the reception. Tony closes the door behind him and his look sends shivers down my spine. He wastes no time placing his lips back on mine.

There's no more reserve in his kiss, no more holding back. The thought that we don't have to anymore…that this vow we have made to each other says he is mine and I am his…It makes my heart leap with joy. We've waited so long for this moment to break down the final walls between us; where two become one. My heartbeat quickens with his. His kisses move down to my neck and then to my collarbone.

A knock on the door makes me jump. Tony raises his head back up to meet mine.

"Later," he tells me and it's all I can do not to speed this reception up and get the heck out of here. He lets me go. He's breathless as he answers the door. Thankfully, he doesn't open it all the way, because I'm still pretty hot and bothered.

I can hear Connor's voice on the other side. "Hey man, I know y'all are now married and all but…yeah… you've got a cake to cut."

I bite my knuckle to keep from laughing as Tony slams the door in Connor's face. He walks back over to me, cupping my face with his hands.

He sighs. "Well, we've waited this long. What's a few more hours?"

I blush and laugh. He's right. Let's enjoy tonight. Enjoy the fact that all of our family and friends that can be with us are here. We'll dance the night away and relish every detail…and then…when it's all said and done, we'll truly become husband and wife.

I nod and Tony grabs my hand once more.

"Good luck trying to figure this dress out," I quip as we walk out the door. "It took three girls to get it on and buttoned."

Tony gives me a heated stare. "I have scissors," he says playfully.

Tony hands me off to my dad for the father/daughter dance. "You look so beautiful tonight," he tells me.

I smile back. "Thanks, Dad. You clean up pretty well yourself."

He gives me a small chuckle. "Well, Carrie had a lot to do with it. I wouldn't have known how to assemble this monkey suit if it hadn't been for her. I would have looked like a disfigured penguin."

I can't help but laugh at his banter. "I really like her, Dad," I say simply.

He gets a twinkle in his eye when he talks of her. I can tell he really likes her. "I like her too," my dad says. "I'm glad that you feel the same—it means a lot."

He gives me a small twirl and then wraps his hand back around my waist. "I can't believe this is it," he says, while choking up.

"Dad," I say quickly, trying to keep him from crying. Because if he cries, I will too and then we'll both be a mess. "I'm not going anywhere. I'm just getting married. I will *always* be your little girl." I purse my lips to keep the tears at bay.

He embraces me in a hug as the song comes to an end. "I love you, Willow."

I squeeze him back. "I love you too, Daddy."

"I wuv you too," Sabby says as he comes up and joins our dance by locking onto both of our legs.

"I love you, little brother, so much you don't even know it." I smile down at him.

"Oh, I's knows it." He grins widely.

"There's someone I want you to meet," Erik says to me when I'm making my way to the punch bowl.

He startled me; I hadn't heard him approach. I turn to find an elderly woman with gnarled, aged hands.

"This is Virginia," Erik says.

The older woman takes my hand in hers and places her other hand on top of mine. There's something different about her but I can't place it.

"Willow, it's so lovely to meet you," she says in a sweet voice.

I smile at her. "It's lovely to meet you as well." Her eyes are the color of sea foam. Both lovely and beautiful.

"I believe I have something that you want. Although I can't physically give it to you, I can guide you in how to use it. I think a day like today is as special as any."

My lips part in question. I try not to look confused but I am completely and utterly lost. She must sense this because she smiles in understanding.

"If you don't mind, I would love to talk to you somewhere quiet. With Tony, of course."

Tony walks up beside us and places his hand on the small of my back.

"Do you know about this?" I ask him.

"Of course. This is my gift to you. And of course, Erik is in on it too." I look up at Tony with confusion. How is this lady a gift to me?

Virginia leads us out of the reception hall. I can't help but shake the feeling that I know someone named Virginia…or heard of her.

On the way out, I spot Connor attempting the running man while Claire holds her shaking head in her hands from embarrassment. I bet she's hoping he doesn't pull that stunt on their wedding day. It's only a few months away.

Ending ELE

The night air is warm on my skin. Tony's hand has since wrapped around mine as we slowly walk from the reception venue following Virginia and Erik. Erik has Virginia's arm draped through his as he escorts her slowly to a sitting area surrounded by a small garden. There are two concrete benches outside. Erik and Virginia take one and Tony and I take the other.

Virginia leans forward and takes my hands in hers again. There's a comforting presence about her. Maybe it comes from being her age or maybe it's her sweet spirit. Either way, her grandmotherly presence puts me at ease.

She pats my hand. "Now that Project ELE is behind us and the world is moving forward, I felt like now would be a good time to give you this gift. Until now, I am the only person to possess it. It is quite possibly the most powerful gift of them all, but I trust that you will use it wisely."

I nod my head in acknowledgement. "You can trust me," I say simply, even though I have no idea what she's referring to.

Erik interjects, "Remember when you first came and saw me back at the camp?" I nod my head. "I told you about a power you had yet to possess, saying it wasn't time for you to have it. That it was very powerful." He pauses, giving me time to think. Then it dawns on me.

"Yes! Now I can place it. Virginia was the person you mentioned that had the gift of passing through time. A seer, Audrey, had a vision of what I would do with a gift like that and it wasn't pretty," I say, remembering the conversation.

"Exactly," Erik says. "Now that the past is behind us and the future is looking bright, we asked Audrey to look again and see if now is the right time." Virginia interjects, "Well, it's a good thing that she gave the go ahead because I'm not getting any younger. I turned eighty-seven this spring. I am the only one known to have my gift and we didn't want it to go completely extinct." Virginia looks deep into my eyes. "I trust you, Willow. I know that you can handle this now."

I smile thoughtfully as she says this. I am honored that they think highly enough of me to trust me with such an important responsibility. And obviously to trust Tony with it too.

Erik looks at Virginia, who nods her head. "I think it's time," Virginia whispers to Erik.

He agrees with her and turns to me. "Willow, Virginia would like to walk you through the first time to make sure you understand this gift. We have found that if you connect with someone through physical contact, you are able to travel with them mentally wherever you decide to go. Now there are two very important rules you must follow. One, you should not ever, under any circumstances, try to change the path of someone's actions. You never know how it will affect the future. Two, you should always take someone with you when you utilize the gift in the instance your emotions overtake your decision making."

Erik takes a deep breath and looks me dead in the eye. "I know how close you were to your mother…"

Ending ELE

A lump forms in my throat as I realize what's about to happen. Tears spill over my cheeks as I choke back sobs. Something I never thought would be possible. I will get a chance to see my mother. I can hear Tony trying to hold back his emotion beside me as he squeezes me tightly against him.

I hold my hand up to Erik, "Give me just a moment, please."

He nods his head, giving me an understanding look. I let my emotions go and cry for a few moments, letting the new emotions I'm feeling calm me. I simply cannot fathom that I will get to see my mother again. I choke back the last few sobs and pull myself together. To hell with my makeup—*I'm going to see my mother*. The thought is still difficult for me to grasp. It feels like I lost her all over again and now I can find her.

I take a deep breath and look over at Tony. He gives me a bittersweet smile and then nods his head in approval.

"It will be the three of you making this journey, Willow: Virginia, Tony, and you."

Virginia takes over the conversation. "I will be there with you the entire time. Now, you can talk to the person. Sometimes they will believe who you are and accept it and sometimes they get scared and run away. You can talk to them and carry on a conversation with them. However, you are able to manipulate a situation by warning them or telling them to do something against their own will. That is what has to be avoided and that is exactly what can change history as we know it. Once you have changed history, it can never be fixed. I'm sure you realize the importance of understanding that last part."

I nod my head eagerly in anticipation.

"Your mother will most likely forget the encounter soon after we leave. Her soul will never forget it, but her mind will. Now, I want us to all link arms. From my experience, you can move about in the vision and it will not change the fact that our arms are linked. If for some reason someone lets go in the vision, they will be pulled from it as well, leaving the person on their own inside the vision."

Again, I nod my head in understanding, trying to feel the weight in each of her words. To really understand everything she is saying.

Virginia leans back over to Erik, whispering something in his ear. He nods.

I glance over to Tony.

"It's going to be fine," he tells me.

I nod my head because words are completely lost on me for this moment.

"Are you ready?" Virginia asks me in her sweet voice.

I take a deep breath and regain my composure. "Yes," I whisper nervously.

She smiles back at me. "Okay then." She takes my hand and squeezes it. "It's time."

My stomach does butterflies in anticipation. I still can't believe this is actually happening.

Erik gets up from the bench and Virginia pats the seat next to her. Both Tony and I move to sit on each side of her. She tells us to link arms, which we do.

"Now, take a deep breath, Willow, and try to remember a time when your mother would have been by herself. It's often easier that way. If not, any good memory will do. I need you to focus on her. Clear your mind of anything else. Pretty soon, you're going to see a white light out of the corner of your eye. You are going to mentally move towards it. Let me know when you see it," Virginia says in a slow and calm voice, much like a hypnotists.

I concentrate on my mother. It's not hard at all to remember her smile and loving heart. I focus on a memory that's more recent since Tony will be with me. I want him to be able to interact with my mother as well. I focus on the time back when we came out of the shelter. I was put in a room to rest and my mother was with me, so was Tony and Mr. Leroy—I mean Lee.

My mother had yelled at Lee to leave the room and then it was just the three of us. I figured I had a better chance for my mother to communicate with me after I told her about my multiple abilities. We didn't get a whole lot of alone time after that.

I focus on the way she held my hand as she listened to me talk about what was happening inside the shelter—and then I see it—the white light that lines the edge of my vision. I mentally move towards it. It takes me a moment to do so, but when I finally figure out how, it goes quickly.

"Okay, I'm there," I tell Victoria. I feel her faintly squeeze my arm. "Good girl. Now just follow that through and then, well, it's hard to explain, you'll materialize into the scene and everything around you and your mother will disappear."

I keep my focus on the light and follow it through. At the end of the light, I see the drab color of the hotel walls come into view. I then see my mother sitting on the bed, holding my hand in hers. It's very weird to see yourself in third person. I also see Tony standing nearby, looking as handsome as ever and slightly younger. We reach the room in full view and everything but my mother disappears, the background becoming a hazy white. It takes a moment for my mother's attention to deviate from the old me on the bed. Tears spring to my eyes as she turns her attention to me.

"Talk to her, but don't startle her," Virginia says.

I look to my left and find her sitting next to me in the vision. Tony sits to my right. I turn my attention back to my mother as she squints her eyes at me. I guess trying to see if what she's seeing is real.

"Mom," I say, my voice breaking, being so overcome with emotion. "Mom, it's me, Willow." I take a deep breath. Here goes nothing. "Mom, I know this is hard to understand but we're from the future. One of the gifts I get much later on is the gift of traveling through time."

I watch her face as she processes this information. "If you're from the future, then why are you coming to see me? Why not just talk to the present me?" she asks curiously.

I think about this for a moment, not knowing if I can disclose the fact that she is no longer with us. "Mom,

I can't tell you that. But if you're having a hard time with this, ask me a question. Ask me a question that no one else would know in a million years but me."

She thinks about this for a moment and then a smile comes to her face. "Tell me about the first time you lost a tooth."

I return her smile as I retell the story. "I lost it while eating noodles. I was so surprised when it fell out onto my plate. At first, I screamed and then I was jumping up and down. You told me the story about the tooth fairy and mine was named Glenda. Then you asked me what I wanted Glenda to bring me for losing my very first tooth. I told you beef jerky and you laughed but said okay. I remember waking up the next morning with a paper bag of jerky and five dollars. I thought I had won the lottery." I smile at her and she smiles back.

A moment passes before I ask her, "Mom, can I give you a hug now?"

She opens her arms to me and I waste no time wrapping my arms around her. I hold her tight, never wanting to let go. I've wished for a moment like this for so long. But now that it's here, I wish for a million more just like it.

She rubs my hair as I cry onto her shoulder. "It's okay, sweet girl. I'm right here."

Eventually I let her go, but not without tremendous effort on my part. I look into her eyes. I had almost forgotten about Tony and Virginia being with me. I look to Tony and my mom follows my line of sight.

"Anthony, it's nice to see you as well. You're still as handsome and strong as ever I see."

He gives her a soft laugh. "Yes ma'am."

She pulls him in for a hug; I guess their formalities of before are thrown out the window.

After they've had their greeting, she says to me, "And this one, I'm not sure if I know…"

I turn to Virginia. "Mom, this is Virginia. She is here with me because this was my first time using this gift and she wanted to make sure everything went smoothly."

My mother holds her hand out to Virginia and she envelopes it with both of her hands.

"It's a pleasure to meet you," Virginia says sweetly. My mother smiles back at her.

Virginia says to me, "We should probably be getting back soon. We can't stay in the past for very long."

My heart plummets in my chest. I can't leave her again—I just found her. I swallow back the tears that threaten to tumble down my face and turn back to my mother.

"Mom, I just want to let you know how much I love you and that everything is going to be okay." I swallow hard and my mother gives me another hug.

When we pull away, I notice that Tony and Virginia are not in the room anymore. It's just my mom and me.

"I got married today, Mom," I say to her, still unsure if that's too much information to divulge.

My mother puts her hand to her mouth in surprise.

"I can't tell you who," I say, knowing that is the

question she wants to ask the most, "but I know that you'd approve. Dad certainly does," I say.

I can see her eyes dance at the mention of my father—her husband.

"There's so much more that I want to tell you but I can't—or I'm not supposed to. It can apparently change the whole time-continuum and all."

She nods her head in confused understanding and takes my hands in hers, the feeling so familiar yet so foreign. "He's one lucky man. Just be sure he treats you well." Her motherly advice, however simple, makes my heart soar. I had missed her so much in the preparations for the wedding. I am just so grateful that I can see her now, on my wedding night. This day is officially complete now.

I realize that our time is coming to an end. With the difficulty of walking through quick sand, I start to say my final goodbyes. "Mom, I just wanted to let you know how much I love you and how thankful I am that you're my mother," I say, careful not to reveal something I may regret. "I have to go now. Thanks for taking care of me."

She smiles at me. "Always." She still seems surprised by the whole visit, which makes sense since I'm lying in a bed in the same room. For me, I haven't seen her in ages. For her, she hasn't even left my bedside.

"Oh, and don't tell my present self in the bed about this. I may—no, I *will* get freaked out and won't be ready to hear it."

She gives me a small laugh. "Not to worry, your secret is safe with me,"

"Thanks, Mom," I say, and I believe her.

With a heavy heart, I let her hands go and say goodbye. *I'll see you again soon*, I think to myself. *In heaven, where I'll never have to say goodbye.* And with that, the vision dissipates and I'm back on the bench, but this time by myself. I look up to find tears in Virginia and Tony's eyes.

"Thank you," I say to them. It goes unmentioned that the thank you is for the few private minutes they allotted me with my mother. I dry off my tears and Tony helps me to my feet. I embrace Virginia in a hug and thank her profusely. I thank Erik the same and they go off to leave Tony and me alone.

"That had to be the best present anyone could have ever given me," I say to him aloud.

He smiles and wipes another tear that escaped my eye. "You're so beautiful," he says to me in that deep, intimate voice of his.

I blush and my head drops. He never ceases to leave me speechless.

"Are you ready to go cut the cake?" he asks.

I smile back up at him. "Absolutely."

Claire and Connor are waiting next to the cakes. The bridal cake is gorgeous with three tiers of red-velvet cake with buttercream icing. The groom's cake is all chocolate and has the look of a white tux detailed in white chocolate on the top. They both look so pretty I kind of despise the thought of cutting into them. Then I come to my senses and grab the cake-cutting knife.

"Make sure you cut from the top," Connor says before he snaps his two fingers. I look over to see Alec on the other side of the room, dimming the lights. I get confused as to why they had to do it but just go with it.

Everyone gathers around to watch us cut the cake. We make the first slice together and I wipe the icing from my finger on his nose. He laughs and wipes it off with a napkin. Both of us cut a piece of each of our cakes, the brides and grooms, and get a forkful.

Connor excitedly interjects, "Don't forget the time honored tradition of feeding the other the first piece!"

I laugh at his energy and nod my head in understanding. *I think he's more excited about the cake than we are*, I think to myself.

Turning my attention back to Tony, I pick up a bite for him and he does the same for me. We both open wide and accept the other's morsel.

Mmmm, chocolate, I think. It's so velvety and smooth. I could probably eat that entire cake in one sitting, so long as no one watched me.

Tony, on the other hand, has the most disgusted look on his face as he chews his cake. It doesn't take him two seconds before he spits out what I gave him on the ground.

My face goes white at his brashness. What on earth…? But before I can form a thought, he pipes in in my head, *"That's not cake—that's pickled beets!"*

I put my hand over my mouth but bust out

laughing anyway. It doesn't take a genius to figure out what just happened.

I look over to Connor, who is laughing hysterically. "I told you I'd get you back!" he yells.

Seeing the look on Tony's face, Connor bolts in the opposite direction. Tony jumps over the entire table and takes off after him. Connor doesn't get far with Tony's speed to his advantage, before he's tackled to the ground, getting a fistful of 'cake' shoved in his mouth.

Claire saunters over next to me.

"Did you know he was going to do that?" I asked her comically while watching the boys wrestle each other.

Claire just shakes her head. "Nope."

We can't suppress the laughter anymore. I give her a hug and we laugh in each other's arms. "Thanks for being the best friend anyone could ever ask for, Claire Bear," I tell her when I calm down enough to talk.

She squeezes me even harder. "Dido, super woman."

~The End~

Eye colors and the abilities they correlate to:

Dark Green- Ability to read minds and hear thoughts. (Willow's first gift. Willow's original eye color: brown. Willow also absorbs other people's gifts when she is around them for a certain period of time. They still don't know how this is possible but some believe it's because she has a bit of Reaper in her. However, there is one major difference between Willow and a Reaper: Willow is still in touch with her humanity.)

Dark Blue- Ability to heal. (Alec's gift. Alec's original eye color: Emerald Green)

Hazel-yellow/green- Ability to compel people and make them do or believe what you tell them. (Zack's gift. Zack's original eye color: light brown)

Purple- Ability to turn invisible (Claire's gift. Claire's original eye color: icy blue)

Brown- Ability to change molecular structure and walk or pass through objects. (Connor's gift. Connor's original eye color- black)

Light Blue- Ability to see through people's abilities

or see when someone is using a gift. (Candy's gift. Candy's original eye color: light brown)

Neon Yellow- Ability to possess great strength, speed, agility and immunity. Rarely, if ever, does someone with this ability get sick. (Willow's mom, whose name is Alice, Sebastian and Tony's gift. As well as everyone else in the first compound. Alice and Sebastian's original eye color: Baby Blue. Tony's original eye color: Hazel Green.

Copper Orange- Ability to see visions of the near future. This is an ability that is new to everyone. Nobody knows how far in the future this ability will allow it's possessor to see, but currently Willow's dad has only been able to see a few minutes and no more than an hour ahead of time. In addition, with the knowledge of what lies ahead, they have been able to change the future outcome. For example, Willow didn't die during the attack on the hotel like the dad foresaw. (Willow's dad: Henry's gift.)

Black- Ability to read other people's emotions and intentions. In addition, this ability allows the possessor to control the emotions of others. (Erik's gift.)

Red- Reapers steal other people's abilities and drain their life from them. Not a lot is known about this power. Some believe that once a Reaper takes from someone that they only possess the ability for a limited period of time. This requires them to continually search for abilities to consume or in other words to help them power up. Because the process of reaping takes a lot of energy and a few minutes to completely drain a person, they don't bother using their powers on the people with yellow eyes.

After all, the Reapers currently possess this ability since it was their first gift before they took the red shot that was supposed to cause instant death. Instead, that shot caused the death of their humanity.

Gold- Telekinesis. Ability to move objects with one's mind. (Marya and John's gift.)

Grey/Silver- Ability to shield oneself from other gifts. Like a force field to other's abilities. (Jennifer's gift.)

White- Allows the person with the gift to see the entire life story of the other person with a single touch. It also causes them to go blind. In Morgan's case, he had his wife, Audrey, help him see. (Morgan's gift, Erik's brother)

Sea Foam- Can travel into the past. (Virgina's gift.)

Blue-Green- Magnetism, draws people to them. (Michael's gift.)

We would love to hear from you! Please come visit us:

Facebook:
http://www.facebook.com/eleseries

Twitter:
Courtney: http://www.twitter.com/nuckelsc
Rebecca: http://www.twitter.com/midnitebeckie

Webpage:

http://www.eleseries.com

ABOUT THE AUTHORS

Rebecca and Courtney are downhome country girls powered by chocolate and other random late night cravings. Coined in southern twang they bring new meaning to the word y'all. BFI's since the 6th grade, with a knack for getting into sticky situations, has resulted in countless ideas to write about for years to come.

ACKNOWLEDGEMENTS

Wow, God has blessed us to be able to do something that before had only been a pipe dream. We had no idea when we started on this adventure that we would finish one book, let alone four books. We are extremely grateful for the success he has granted us and for his biggest blessing of all, our Lord Jesus. *(Philippians 4:13)*

We appreciate all of the support we have received from book blogs, our favorite Facebook pages, our family and friends and most of all from our fans. Your encouragement kept us writing. All of your Facebook posts, Goodreads comments and emails that told us that you loved our books, made our hearts soar and made us want to write even better for you. Thank you to everyone who has taken the time to review our book and thank you to everyone who continues to read our work. A shout out to Cynthia Shepp for doing wonders for our story. You really do have a way with words!

To Marya Heiman with Strong Image Editing: Have we told you how much we love you today?!? Words cannot express our gratitude for all you do. We just can't thank you enough. Where would we be without you?

Last but not least: a giant thank you to our Awesome Sauce Street Team who are out there on the front lines helping us spread the word about our books. We love you all! Carly Bel-air, Claire Taylor, Lauren Harrington, Brenna Harden, Jamie Cross, Ashley Wiggins, Ashley Wood, Mia Melone, Veronica Morfi, Laura Martinez, Angela Stone, Terri Dion, Kim Culbertson, Shona Lawrence, Lauren Dootson, Dyan Brown, Cynthia Shepp, Kendall McCubbin, Lela Lawing, Kathleen Guardado, Tonya Bunch, Lisa Sasso, Natlie Idrogo, Heather Alexander, Brittany Willis, Marya Heiman, Melanie Newton, Alicia Hall, Amy Stogner, Colleen Reilly, Jovhanna Caltzontzi, Kristy Hamilton, Rebekah Ashworth, Heather Piantanida-pipes, Michele Skinner, Cassie Hoffman, Kristin Kim, Nikki Archer, Irayda Quezada, Karissa Stephens, Jamie Miller, Krystal Marlein, Pam Mandigo, Melanie Martin, Lori Fenn, Mayra Arellano, Cassie Chavez, Samantha Trusdale and Jamie Cross. These names are in no particular order. You are all amazing and we are so grateful to have you!

CPSIA information can be obtained
at www.ICGtesting.com
Printed in the USA
LVHW01s2325120218
566358LV00001B/17/P